By Dean Murray

The Destroyer

Dean Murray

Published by Fir'shan Publishing

ISBN 978-1-9393635-8-9

www.FirshanPublishing.com

First Edition

For Lachele

Chapter 1

"My name really is Tyrell, but you would probably know me better as the Destroyer."

The last thing I expected was to believe those words, but I did. It didn't make any sense—everything I had ever been taught pointed to the Destroyer, the man who'd fractured the world nearly beyond repair, being dead for more than a hundred and fifty years.

Even if the recorded histories were all wrong and he hadn't died while trying to destroy the Founder, even with nanite technology—the technology that he'd helped create—human life expectancy was only slightly more than a hundred years. All of the records agreed that the Destroyer had been well into middle age when he'd created the first viable nanites.

Just based on that, he should have been dead for the better part of a hundred years—only I was becoming more and more convinced with every passing day that the things I'd been taught on the other side of the barrier weren't true.

For starters, it had been accepted by every member of the Society that nanite technology was only available to the franchised citizens on our side of the barrier—the massive energy field which protected our homes from the rest of the world, or as we liked to call them, the grubbers. Only I'd just been defeated in hand-to-hand combat by a man who I was convinced was not a Society operative. My nanites gave me speed and strength that were quite literally inhuman. The only way Tyrell could have possibly defeated me—let alone in such a decisive manner—was if he also had nanites.

Not just any nanites either. Before I'd left the safety of the barrier to come stop what I thought was an egotistical warlord from developing a doomsday weapon, I'd been injected with what the Citizen-President himself had told me was a cutting-edge, prototype strain of nanites that drastically exceeded the capabilities of even the nanite packs given to the Society military personnel.

I'd tested myself against those military personnel and confirmed the difference in our capabilities, but it very much appeared that my nanites were at least a generation or two behind the ones flowing through Tyrell's blood. As I looked up at Tyrell, who was poised to crush my throat, I felt like a computer program that had just run into something it had never been designed to handle.

I could either let myself break by refusing to accept the reality I found myself in, or I could accept that the impossible was actually possible.

Oddly enough, once I realized that one of the foundational precepts upon which my life had been built was a lie, it became surprisingly easy to question everything else I'd ever been told.

Members of the Society, franchised and non-franchised citizens alike, had been taught that we were fired upon first during the Desolation—the worldwide war during which more than eighty percent of the population perished. Shortly after I'd arrived inside the city, Brennan—the supposedly egotistical warlord I'd been sent to stop—had told me that the Society had it all wrong. We hadn't been fired upon first, we'd been the ones who'd started the war.

Given that Brennan, Tyrell, and everyone else I'd met so far inside the compound were just focused on surviving, it was hard to believe that they were the warmongers I'd been led to believe they were. Especially not considering that the Citizen-President had parked one of the Society's mammoth mobile command centers above the city with orders to level everything outside the compound so that he could send in ground troops to steal Brennan's greatest invention.

Knowing that I'd been lied to—probably thousands of times—made the choice of whether to trust the Citizen-President easy, but it didn't help me when it came to knowing what to tell Tyrell in order to keep him from taking my life.

Fortunately Brennan, the gorgeous, dark-haired, seventeen-year-old warlord who I'd risked everything to rescue just hours earlier, arrived before Tyrell could do anything else.

"Tyrell, what are you doing? Get off of her!"

Given the gravity of my situation, I didn't swoon like I might have under other circumstances, but that didn't stop me from being incredibly happy that he hadn't somehow been injured or abducted again while I'd been recovering from my rescue attempt. Before I could decide what to say, Tyrell responded to Brennan's question.

"She came here intending on assassinating you, Brennan. It's the only explanation for why she'd choose to blow her cover."

I shook my head desperately. "That's not it at all. I never would have risked everything to save Brennan from Piter if I'd had any intention of killing him."

Tyrell had never looked away from me—not even when Brennan opened the vault-like door leading up from his workshop—but now his eyes went even colder. "You're not even going to deny being one of their agents? You've been lying to us for days—you can't honestly expect us to believe anything you tell us now."

"You're right, I'm an operative. I was sent here to stop Brennan from weaponizing his generator. I was told that he was creating it to power some kind of energy weapon that would be capable of bringing down the barrier."

Tyrell's fist tightened around my neck. "And by stop Brennan, you mean assassinate him."

"No! I mean it was a possibility, but only a very remote one. I was told that Brennan was no better than the likes of Piter, and my briefings all indicated that it was a miracle Brennan had managed to get the components required to build the generator in the first place. I came here believing I could destroy the generator—I thought that would remove the threat for good."

Before Tyrell could respond, Brennan cut in. "Let her up, Tyrell. She's right, it would make no sense for her to kill me now—not after saving my life twice."

"We've talked about this, Brennan. She saved you from Jerome to gain your trust. It doesn't mean what you think it means. Alexander never would've sent her here to actually destroy the generator. He needs it too badly to ever let that happen. She's lying."

Brennan shook his head. "Maybe you're right, old friend, but that doesn't explain why she would've come after me last night. She already had my confidence, and with me out of the way—which is exactly what would've happened if she hadn't come for me—it would've been that much easier for the ants to swoop in and take the generator."

The two of them were talking too quickly for me to get a word in edgewise. I tried, but Tyrell had already responded.

"You're still thinking like you, Brennan, rather than like the parasite who's been feeding on the people living behind that energy shield for all these decades. If you got your hands on partially finished technology like your generator, you would do whatever it took to figure out the principles it'd been designed to operate on. The ants—Alexander—don't have anyone capable of something like that. Even if they did, they would never actually get it working given that their resident genius would refuse to work more than an hour or two per week."

Brennan sighed. "Maybe you're right, Tyrell, but we're never going to know for sure whether we can trust Skye unless we give her the ability to betray us. Let her up."

"You still don't understand what you're dealing with, Brennan. Skye isn't running the version two nanites that the ants' military personnel are injected with. She's got Alexander's own nanites circulating through her blood. They aren't a match for mine—even before my last several rounds of modifications—but they are far and away better than anything else you've come up against. Even with the nanite injections I've been giving you, she's still more than capable of killing you in a heartbeat. You would never even see the attack coming."

Brennan walked over and pried Tyrell's hand off of me. "We're running out of options, Tyrell. Right now there's a mobile command center floating above the city. We knew that was going to be Alexander's response eventually once word of my generator got out, but now that Katya has gone dark we don't have any kind of escape route out of here."

Brennan couldn't have really made Tyrell let go of me—not given just how strong Tyrell's nanites made him. Tyrell had released me willingly, but you wouldn't have known it to look at him.

"We still have options."

"No, we don't. We don't know how long we have until the assault starts."

I cleared my throat. "It was supposed to start within the next hour or two, but I convinced the Citizen-President to delay it twenty-four hours."

Brennan looked hopeful, but Tyrell still just looked suspicious. "How did you manage that?"

"I told him that I could lure the bulk of your security forces to one spot so that they could take them out with a single strike."

Tyrell opened his mouth—probably to say something snide—but this time I beat him to the punch. "I lied to him to buy you as much time as possible, and then I ran straight here to warn you. I know that I've lied to both of you—to everyone inside the compound—but I'm not lying this time. Too many things aren't adding up. That mobile command center shouldn't be here. It should have required a vote of every franchised citizen in the entire Society, but nobody asked me and the president didn't say anything about a vote when I talked to him.

"My mission was supposed to be a simple destruction of prohibited technology, but now it's somehow turned into some kind of smash-and-grab. Throw in the fact that Tyrell obviously has nanites of his own, and you're healing nearly as quickly as if you have nanites as well, and it's looking like I've been lied to over and over again by the Citizen-President and nearly everyone else."

"I can see that Brennan's nearly ready to believe you, Skye, but I'm not. You didn't know about my nanites when you made your last radio transmission, and the rest of your reasons seem awfully thin for someone who's spent their entire life on the other side of the barrier."

I felt myself starting to blush. I didn't want to admit that I had feelings for Brennan, but my very life depended on Tyrell and Brennan believing that I was telling them the truth. The best way to make sure that they believed me was to actually tell the truth.

"I...it's hard to explain. You don't know what it's like to grow up over there and then be shown this world. My entire life I've been told that there's only one correct way of doing things. You're doing exactly the opposite of the things that I've been told lead to happiness, and yet the people living here inside of the compound seem genuinely happy.

"Now that I've been here it all just makes sense. How can someone be happy wasting ninety percent of their time? You've given your people something meaningful to work towards, and they are happily putting in twelve-hour days working towards that goal. A year ago this compound didn't even exist, but now it does—and it's amazing.

"Back home, we're told that we're making incredible progress, but that isn't the case. You started with so much less, but you've come so much further. It makes me think that all of the problems out here in the cities aren't because the people aren't following the precepts, it's because they're lacking the leadership to show them how to deal with the corruption and violence."

My face continued to heat up and I looked away, unable to meet Brennan's eyes. "Most of all though, what the Citizen-President wants to do to you feels wrong. Back home the Citizen-President is a model citizen, the perfect leader, but you never would even consider bombing an enemy—a weaker enemy at that—without talking to them first. You wouldn't bomb *anyone* unless you didn't have any other option. I gave the

Citizen-President another option. I told him I could make sure that the generator would never be weaponized, but it was like I wasn't even speaking. I don't want to be working for a man like that, not when I could be working for one like you."

It was dangerously close to an admission of my growing feelings towards Brennan, but I couldn't see any way to avoid at least saying that much. Brennan looked at Tyrell expectantly.

"You already know how I feel, old friend. The things she's just told us don't change anything for me. I believe her, and if it were up to me, I'd have already injected her with a few cc's of your blood. The only question is whether or not you can trust her enough to include her in your plans."

Tyrell held Brennan's gaze for several seconds before seeming to arrive at a decision. "I'm going to tell you what actually happened a hundred and fifty years ago. Once you know the truth, your response will determine whether or not you'll leave this room alive."

Chapter 2

Somehow Tyrell's ultimatum didn't surprise me. The same couldn't be said of Brennan. "Absolutely not! We had a deal, Tyrell. I'm the one who gets to decide what's an acceptable risk where my own life is concerned. You went along with having her around me all by herself for days now. You don't get to just up and kill her now after all of that."

"Yes, we did have a deal—we do have a deal—but the situation has changed more than you realize. I wasn't worried about Skye killing you when she first arrived because I knew that Alexander wanted your generator, and he was smart enough to realize he couldn't get that if you died before you finished it."

"We've been over this twice already since I got back. She wouldn't have—"

"Yes, we have been over it, but you don't seem to understand that her saving you from

Piter's men could have been nothing more than her following orders. Alexander knows that the generator's not finished yet."

"If the Citizen-President knew that and sent me in to save Brennan, then why would he send in a mobile command center to level the city just hours later? Actually, that's not even the right question, that mobile command center had to be on its way days ago. When I set off to save Brennan, the Citizen-President already knew that the mobile command center was just about to arrive at the city."

The words had just slipped out of my mouth without any real thought on my part, but they were the right words. I was actually impressed with myself, even more so with my delivery. I hadn't sounded scared or angry, I'd just stated the facts.

Apparently that dispassionate approach was the way to go. At least it seemed to have gotten Tyrell's attention. He opened his mouth to respond, but once again I calmly talked over him.

"Go ahead and tell me what happened, Tyrell. I didn't come here tonight to kill Brennan, but regardless of whether or not you believe me, I still want to hear the truth."

"Very well, I'll start at the beginning. By the time that I met your 'Founder,' I had been working on developing nanotechnology for nearly two decades. It was an exciting time, a time that people nowadays can't even fathom. Everything was changing so quickly that there wasn't any way to keep up with all the developments in all the different fields, but nothing was as promising as what I was working on.

"By the time I met your Founder, nanites were a reality. We had managed to build tiny machines that were capable of incredible tasks. Curing cancer wasn't just a possibility, it was a reality. It was widely acknowledged that there wasn't anything relating to the human body that couldn't be accomplished with enough time and money."

"They were too expensive, weren't they?"

I couldn't have said exactly where my observation came from. We had always been told inside the Society that the creation of nanites was expensive. That was the justification for making people work so hard in order to earn their franchise—only after living in Brennan's compound, I realized that earning a franchise was a ridiculously trivial undertaking.

Whatever my reasons for opening my mouth, for once Tyrell didn't seem angry with me. "Yes, you're exactly right. The early nanite prototypes were incredibly expensive to manufacture. It was creating unfathomable stress on societies all around the world. The truly wealthy individuals were buying their way into research projects, funding the research in exchange for custom-built nanites designed to cure whatever their particular malady was.

"For the first time in decades, there was a very real difference in the quality of healthcare being received by different individuals in First World countries, and insurance companies wouldn't have touched nanite treatments even if they had been commercially available. There were…riots…breaking out all over the world as people were forced to watch their loved ones dying from conditions that could've been cured if only they'd been part of the wealthiest tenth of a percent of the population."

For a moment, Tyrell looked off into space. "Those of us who worked in the field were sequestered inside of secure compounds for our own safety, but there wasn't anything they could do to shield us from the things people were saying about us. My colleagues and I were insulted in every conceivable manner by the very people we were trying to save, but I forced myself not to let it affect me. I knew that we were getting close, that the real prize was just around the corner.

"We could save lives if given enough lead time to map someone's body and produce the nanites required to heal them, but even the wealthiest individuals couldn't afford to produce nanites in the quantities required to stop them from aging. I knew achieving that would change the very fabric of life all across the planet, but it also had the chance of destroying entire nations. People were already angry that their medical treatments weren't as good as what the rich received, they would only become even more desperate once they realized immortality was on the line."

"You figured it out though, right? I mean, you've got to be more than two hundred years old at this point; that's pretty compelling evidence that you cracked whatever problem was stopping you back then."

"Yes, I figured out what needed to change. Rather than treating the nanites like a sophisticated kind of antibiotic, something to be injected into the body to perform a single task before shutting down and being expelled through natural means, we needed to treat the nanites like a symbiotic organism.

"I developed plans and models that would allow the nanites themselves to map their host body, completely eliminating the need for expensive imaging and modeling prior to someone receiving a nanite injection. Once I was convinced that would work, I proceeded to design a new kind of nanite, one with a fraction of the storage capacity of previous models. Rather than programming them during the manufacturing process, I envisioned a nanite that was capable of receiving and executing instructions on an ongoing basis."

I cleared my throat. "The computer node and the transmitting rings."

"Yes, exactly. And it worked. I did extensive testing on non-human subjects and proved the concept. It brought the cost of nanite treatments down to a small fraction of what they'd been, and it meant that once someone had been treated they would never need another injection. Don't get me wrong, it was still very crude. The computer wasn't capable of monitoring the body in real time, and installing a new set of instructions into memory for transmission to the nanites required surgery, but it was still the kind of technological leap that comes along only once in a century.

"There was a problem though. The host bodies invariably rejected both the computer and the factory after a time, with the result of rejection usually being death."

"How did you solve that problem?"

"I didn't, someone else did. Alex was a rising star in the scientific community. Charming, brilliant, and well-connected. It seemed like there was no area of technology that he hadn't impacted for the better. The breadth of his accomplishments were nothing less than awe-inspiring, so when he approached me with a desire to collaborate on my research I eagerly accepted his offer.

"Alex told me that he'd been following my progress and that he believed there was a way to both stop the rejection of nanite machinery and create an interface between the neural pathways in the host and the nanite computer itself. It was the kind of collaboration that legends are made out of. I brought the ability to create machines that could in turn create other machines, while he provided the last piece of the puzzle required to make nanites economical for mass injection into the general public."

Something that Brennan had said just a minute or two earlier clicked into place for me.

"You used the human body as the ultimate nanite factory."

"Yes, indeed. We were careful never to come right out and admit our plan in that area, but even so we still received a firestorm of criticism from our contemporaries. They had a million reasons why our plan was irresponsible, but for each of their reasons we had a valid counter. They worried about the spread of communicable diseases, but I was confident that our nanites would make infectious diseases a thing of the past. They were afraid we were about to unleash a plague of self-aware microscopic robots on humanity, but we had already proved that our nanites were incapable of surviving outside of the human body for more than a short period of time.

"We moved forward in secret, operating on an accelerated timetable that was only possible because the nanites in our test subjects reported back on their condition in real-time. A short time later, we injected ourselves with the first part of the treatment, a genetic serum designed by Alex which rewired the immune system so that it would not reject the nanite implants, and then there was nothing to stop us from injecting ourselves with a foundational layer of nanites designed to build the computer and factory that would allow us to iterate to nanites capable of bestowing immortality on their host."

We were approaching the critical juncture of the story, but I managed to keep my mouth shut so that Tyrell could continue to tell it in his own way.

"I was so blindingly happy with the progress we were making that I largely ignored the warning signs. Alex was unable to adjust his serum beyond a very narrow range. It meant that the burden of most of the changes required to get our solution working fell on the hardware side—on me. Not only that, he was secretive about his process for developing the serum, and he was much less brilliant than I'd been led to believe. He seemed to have an adequate understanding of both our fields, but I never saw him make the kind of intuitive leaps that are the defining characteristic of a true genius.

"I've replayed those last few months in my mind thousands of times wishing that I'd been more perceptive, but I wasn't. I played into his hands like the fool that I'd come to believe he was. Don't get me wrong, Alex didn't invent any of the discoveries with which he was credited, but he was no fool.

THE DESTROYER

"He'd made a career out of separating unprepared geniuses like me from their greatest discoveries. Even before we started working together, he'd been planning on stealing my half of the nanite technology, and I would've given it to him but for sheer dumb luck. We had both injected ourselves with our creation, but I was the one doing all the work when it came to designing new strains of nanites."

Tyrell smiled in remembered joy from a better time. "Those were heady, exciting times. I would create a new design, upload it to the computer inside my body, and then let the computer reprogram the nanites to modify themselves or the neural-mechanical interface. It meant that I could test out new iterations to my nanites at lightning speed, but it also meant that I was working without a safety net. The wrong design, a stray line of code, an errant transmission, any of those things could have resulted in my nanites malfunctioning and killing me, but I managed to avoid all of that and create a set of programs and designs that succeeded in halting the aging process inside of my body.

"I remember being so excited. I called Alex down to my laboratory and injected him with a vial of my blood, a vial full of nanites that I'd ordered to rebuild the relevant systems inside of his body so that his computer and nanite factory would be able to grant him the gift of immortality."

The smile from a moment before was gone now. "It was the fastest way to make those kinds of changes because I'd been very careful to lock down each of our nanite computers with complicated security measures. It wasn't something I expected to need with Alex, but even then I was looking forward to the future where our discoveries were commonplace."

"You didn't want people to be able to hack other people's computers. You were worried they could use someone's nanites as the perfect murder weapon."

"Yes, I was. I knew that injections were inherently less dangerous because the victim's own nanites could be instructed to fight off any aberrant behavior. I injected him with nanites that provided him with a computer capable of more accurately controlling his own nanites, but never uploaded the program that would've allowed his computer to instruct his own nanites to do the same thing for someone else."

"He tried to kill you, didn't he?"

"Yes, he did. He nearly succeeded, but in the end he underestimated the regenerative abilities of my nanites and walked off having failed to finish the job. I've been fighting him ever since."

Everything clicked into place and I realized the answer had been staring me in the face ever since I'd realized that Tyrell was more than two hundred years old.

"Alex—the Founder—is still alive, isn't he?"

"Yes, Skye. He is."

Tyrell grimaced, as though in pain, but it took me several seconds to understand why. He was grimacing because he really was in pain. I watched as Tyrell's face shifted, accomplishing a transformation that made the single change my nanites were capable of bestowing on me, look like the child's tool that it really was.

Over the next twenty seconds Tyrell cycled through two more faces before letting his face return to the one he usually wore. When he finally turned back to me, I knew that he was capable of looking like almost anyone.

"Alex—Alexander—is still alive, and he's never left the protection of the barrier. For more than one hundred and fifty years he's maintained control over the people he rules by changing his face so that no one would realize that the elections are rigged. Your Citizen-President is the man who stole the gift of immortality from humanity and then did his best to make sure that no one would ever be able to challenge him."

Chapter 3

I felt like I'd been punched in the stomach. Tyrell's revelation had been staring me in the face my entire life, but I'd never been able to see it. I'd been so caught up in the question of whether my service would eventually earn me my franchise that I'd never stopped to question the way that we held a knife to the throat of every man, woman and child living on the planet outside of our barrier. Even once Tyrell had revealed himself to be the Destroyer, I still hadn't been able to put the pieces together well enough to realize that the Founder had been ruling us since the beginning.

I tried to respond, tried to come up with something I could say that would convince Tyrell I was really on their side, but the shock was simply too great for me to process. I knew that my lack of response might get me killed, but I just couldn't seem to get my voice to work.

THE DESTROYER

Before I could resolve the logjam inside of my mind, one of Jax's soldiers burst into the room. "Sir, I'm sorry to interrupt, but I have a message from my commander. We've been pushed back off the barricade on all four sides of our territory. Commander Jax estimates that we'll be forced back to the compound walls within the next two hours, and he requests your presence at his command center."

Brennan swore and turned as though to leave, but then stopped as he remembered the standoff between Tyrell and me.

"I need to get up there right now, Tyrell, and see if there's anything I can do to stem the tide, but I'm not going to leave Skye here alone with you. She's coming with me."

Tyrell shook his head. "You're our biggest asset. Your place is down in your workshop where I know you're safe. I can go help Jax, but I can't create the scopes we need to turn that new rifle of yours into a real sniper's weapon. We can leave the messenger here to serve as your guard, and I'll take Skye topside with me until we can decide what to do with her. I'm the only one who has any hope of stopping her if she decides to make her move."

Brennan held up a slim black cylinder that I hadn't noticed until that moment. "It's still not working. I just wasted the last hour trying to create a rifle scope, but there's still something wrong with my calculations. We don't have machinery precise enough to do what we're trying to do—at least not for this application. It would take me several weeks still to build the tools we need to create one of these with the accuracy we're after.

"You're the one who's irreplaceable, Tyrell. Even Katya doesn't have the final nanite package. That means if you die, the secret of immortality dies with you. For the sake of the entire human race, we can't risk that. We'll all go up to the surface, but you'll take over the command center and Jax and I will go out and do what we can to hold off the barbarians at our gates. It's the only thing that makes sense."

Tyrell frowned. "I don't have the secret to immortality anymore—I never did. Not without Alexander's anti-rejection serum."

"You don't have the complete secret, but your control computer is the one piece of all of this that can't be reproduced anywhere else on the earth right now. Alexander has been producing his serum behind that barrier for a century and a half, but you and I both know that the nanites he's been giving his people come directly from his body. As long as you're still alive there's a chance that we can get control over his production facilities and change the fate of the human race."

I could see that Tyrell wanted to keep arguing, but in the end he just sighed and nodded. "Very well, I'll take over operations, but Skye stays with me."

"It seems that we're at an impasse. I suggest that we let Skye choose where she wants to go."

"With you. If I have a choice, then I want to do my job. I signed up as your bodyguard and if you're going to be out there in the thick of the fighting then I would like to be watching your back."

I expected Tyrell to go through the roof. He'd been fighting to keep me away from Brennan ever since I'd come back from the rescue operation in Piter's territory, and he'd made it very clear that he didn't trust me outside of his own sight, but Tyrell just nodded.

"Very well. I'm tired of fighting with the two of you. Let's go pick up Skye's transmitter on our way to Jax's command center."

Before we left the dormitory level, Brennan fished out a master key to all of the bedrooms and handed it to the messenger.

"Stay here and make sure nobody tries to get down into my workshop. Once we get to the command center, I'll send a couple of people back to collect that key. If the fighting is going as badly as it sounds like it is, we're going to need to collect the ammo stored in everybody's rooms."

The messenger nodded and then the other three of us set out. It took only a few minutes to get down to where I'd left my transmitter, but Tyrell fidgeted impatiently the entire time we were down in the bore. Brennan tried to convince him that there was no need for him to accompany the two of us, but he steadfastly refused to go on ahead. Instead we traveled with me in the very front of the procession and Tyrell immediately behind me so that he could end my life if I tried any funny business.

"This is it, huh?"

I nodded and handed the hand-sized transmitter over to Brennan. "It just needs to be attached to a big enough piece of metal to serve as the antenna. It's not designed to be able to be used on other channels though, so it will be of limited use to us."

Brennan shrugged. "Maybe if we make it out of all of this I'll pull it apart. I still don't know very much about radios."

There didn't seem to be much else to say, so I turned around and led the way back up to the surface.

I wasn't sure where Jax would've set up his operations, but there were enough messengers running back and forth that it didn't take much to find him. He'd set up just inside the south gate to the compound.

I led our little group into the building and then stood off to one side so as not to be in the way while Brennan, Tyrell, and Jax talked. Jax shook Brennan's hand.

"Despite the fact that you being seen walking around after being nearly dead just a few days ago is going to raise some difficult questions, I'm glad to see the two of you. Things have gotten much worse out there than we expected, and it's time to start making some difficult decisions."

"I guess it's a good thing that I brought Tyrell then. Point me at something that needs to be built and I can get the job done, but when it comes to squad-level tactics, I'm not your guy."

Brennan smiled wryly. "As for your other concern, it can't be helped. As hot as things are getting on the other side of the wall, none of our people are going to be in a position to worry about my recovery any time soon. I'll come up with something to tell them once the dust settles.

"It's probably a good thing that none of them have experienced anything remotely approaching real medical care other than here. That and Tyrell's reputation for working miracles in his hospital just may be enough to deflect attention away from the impossibility of me being back on my feet already."

Tyrell stepped over to a table containing what looked like a crude map of Brennan's territory and rubbed his chin. "You're right, this is a lot worse than I was expecting. What happened?"

"We've pretty much destroyed the entire Muertos gang. I'm sure there are a few of them still gunning for us, but their neighbors have already started moving into the area, which means they are no longer a going concern. In some circumstances they didn't even wait for us to get out of the way before they started annexing the territory. By and large the same kind of thing is happening in Piter's territory as well. The destruction of his forces wasn't as complete as what we managed with the Muertos, but his leadership group was decapitated."

"That was about what we expected. Where did things start going wrong?"

"Apparently Piter did even more priming of our neighbors than we realized. Shortly after dawn we started experiencing probing attacks all along our borders. All I can figure is that the rest of the gang leaders and warlords in the area have decided now is the time to attack in an effort to be the group left standing when all the dust settles."

Brennan muttered something that was probably a curse. "I should've seen this coming. Everybody knows that we've got more than enough firepower to fight off any two or three of our closest rivals, but even we won't be able to defeat everyone on our borders. I thought the destruction of the Muertos and Piter's group would be enough to dissuade everyone from coming after us."

Jax nodded. "It was a reasonable assumption. The leaders of the groups attacking us have to know that their chances of holding our territory once we're dead are very slim."

"Apparently they feel like the prize is worth the risk—that or they just can't risk having our ammunition production facility fall into the hands of their rivals. We were relatively quiet neighbors, but if one of these other groups had an endless supply of ammunition the first thing they would do would be to launch an all-out attack designed to control everything for forty blocks in every direction."

Another guard came running into the room and handed Jax a slip of paper. Jax read the message and sighed.

"We've been pushed back almost all the way to the compound on our western border. Tyrell, if you're going to take over here, then I should probably take a squad and get over there."

"Yes, go ahead and do that. I have a few ideas that may buy us some time."

Jax saluted both Brennan and Tyrell, and then left the room followed by two of his men. Tyrell continued to study the map for several minutes after Jax had left. I was tempted to get closer so that I could see what was going on, but I didn't want Tyrell to think that I was still trying to spy on Brennan's operations. Besides, there was no guarantee that I was going to be able to understand the notes on the map.

Brennan tapped on the table, seemingly lost in thought until he looked up at his mentor. "The first thing we need to do is free up additional manpower to reinforce the places where we're getting pushed back. I know Jax would never approve, but we should recruit runners from nonessential personnel here in the compound and stop using guards to pass messages."

"You're right, Jax would never agree to that. He's right—under normal circumstances it's too risky to have nonmilitary personnel passing critical updates. The messengers could be killed out there, and even if they're not, there's a much bigger chance that we've got spies inside the general populace of the compound than there is that we've got spies inside the guards."

"I don't think we have any other choice. Our odds of surviving this aren't very good as it is, but if we are going to have any chance we have to at least hold the compound for the next twenty-four hours."

Tyrell carefully drew a pair of circles, one inside of each other, both centered on the compound. "That mobile command center is going to want to leave a healthy buffer around the compound when they start destroying the city. Even precision munitions like what they'll be using against us aren't perfectly accurate and they aren't going to want to risk damaging the generator. By my rough math, this inner area here should be safe when those tungsten rods start dropping. The outer band here is the area that they'll be trying to leave undamaged, but which could take some stray strikes.

"That means we need to hold our territory for as long as possible and then fall back into the compound immediately before the strikes arrive. The best-case scenario is that we still have enough people left alive once the strikes have landed to fight off the ants' military when they start bringing in troops."

Brennan nodded, but I got the feeling he wasn't agreeing with quite what Tyrell thought he was agreeing to. He picked up a pencil and drew an 'X' over a building on the southern border. The map was crude enough that I was having a hard time orienting myself with what I knew of the city, but that building seemed familiar. A second later Brennan confirmed my suspicions.

"The parking garage where Victoria's people were training looks like it should be inside of the blast perimeter. I know we can't bring all of the people from outside of the compound in here, but we need to at least give them a chance to hole up inside of this structure."

"There's no way that we can hold two perimeters, Brennan. Trying to do that will just guarantee that we don't have the people we need to put up a real fight when the ants start landing."

"I know you're in charge of operations, but I'm not going to just stand by and let all of those people die, Tyrell. You don't have to try to hold two spots, I'll go out there myself and start sending people that direction. I won't be able to save everybody, but if I get the word out and we can put enough people down there with even just a few rifles, they'll have a real chance of holding off all of those enforcers—especially given that there's nothing of any real value down there. The other warlords are going to be focused on trying to take the compound."

Brennan picked up a spare rifle and started filling his pockets with ammunition while Tyrell watched with a frown. "You know I can't let you throw your life away like this."

Brennan shrugged. "I'm not nearly as valuable as you keep trying to imply. I'm reasonably bright, but other than that, I'm nothing special. The goal of this operation was to draw out Alexander so that we could destroy that mobile command center before all of those troops deployed.

"We've failed there, but the question of whether or not I survive is a pretty minor one. Assuming you somehow make it out of here, it won't take you too much effort to find somebody else with the potential of helping you rebuild the technology that's been lost for all these decades."

"Fine, I'll re-task all of the messengers into a combat role and we'll try to push the enemy forces back to the point where people will be able to move around the compound so that they can go to that parking garage."

"Don't go ruining your chance of survival for me, old man. The most important thing is that once the bombardment stops, you and Jax still have enough guards to have a chance of stealing one of the ants' aircraft."

"I'm very aware of that, but I was going to have to do something like this regardless. We're struggling to hold them off now during the middle of the day when we've got clear sightlines. Things are only going to get worse once it gets dark. We need to buy ourselves room to fall back once the sun sets or we're going to lose the compound walls before the bombardment ever starts. You're going to take the girl?"

"Yeah, Jax isn't going to be happy about me going out there without him, but I'm not so stupid as to think that I don't need some backup. I'll take Skye and whoever else you want to send along."

"There is a reason that I sent Jax off before you and I had this conversation, Brennan. If we're going to hold out—especially if we're going to try to save a significant percentage of the people out there living between the compound walls and the barricade—we need him focused on killing bad guys rather than worrying about watching your back."

"I appreciate the vote of confidence—and I suspect that Skye does as well."

Tyrell shook his head. "I don't like it any more than Jax will when he finds out, but we don't have any choice. You're the equal of any two of Jax's men and after last night it's been pretty conclusively demonstrated that she's the best killer this side of the barrier.

"Just watch yourself. If you get captured we're not going to have the manpower or time, either one, to get you free."

Chapter 4

Tyrell offered Brennan another nanite injection before we left, but Brennan waved the offer away saying that Tyrell needed to save his nanites to get him through what was coming next. Brennan motioned for three of the junior guards outside of the planning room to join us, and we left, headed out the compound's southern gate.

I was dying to find out more, to ask Brennan about his relationship with Tyrell and the injections that he'd been receiving, but I knew it wasn't the time or place for that. We were walking into a war zone with three guards who couldn't be allowed to find out who Tyrell was. The question of how much benefit Brennan received from being injected with nanite-rich blood was going to have to wait.

The latest reports had indicated that we were still well behind the fighting on this front, but that didn't stop us from keeping our weapons ready and our eyes peeled. We traveled in a loose diamond formation with me at the front and Brennan in the middle. Brennan tried to argue with me, but I refused to back down when it came to putting him in the most protected spot we could manage.

He'd convinced Tyrell that he was at least semi-expendable, but I wasn't about to let him die if there was anything I could do to stop it. Not after everything I'd gone through to rescue him, not given the way I felt about him.

After ten minutes of walking, the sound of gunfire was getting close enough that I knew we could be running into enforcers at any point. Despite that realization, it still took me by surprise when I rounded the corner and saw three men with a variety of weapons exiting one of the buildings to my right.

"Put your weapons down and your hands up!"

They'd already taken several steps in the opposite direction by the time I yelled. I was nearly positive that they weren't normal citizens from Brennan's territory, but I didn't want to open fire on them without making sure of that.

The response I got took me completely by surprise. Rather than surrendering, all three of them turned and charged towards me.

My rifle was already tight against my shoulder and my sights settled on the middle enforcer almost of their own accord. I stroked my trigger and a fraction of a second later three bullets tore into the heavyset body that had already covered a surprising amount of ground.

I tracked to the right intending on taking down another of the enforcers, but two bursts of gunfire from behind me stitched red dots across my target's chest. I took down the last enforcer with another three-round burst and then turned to find the two guards on either side of the diamond focused on the street ahead of us.

"You need to stay focused on your quadrant no matter what. You're not just soldiers right now, you're also bodyguards. Based on the way those guys were creeping out of those buildings, they're trying to flank our position up ahead. That means there's no such thing as a front-line. We could get attacked from any direction at any moment—which means you need to be covering your quadrant."

"But there were three of them."

The guard who was speaking looked like he couldn't have been older than fourteen. He was too young for this, but it wasn't like we could be choosy. The war had arrived long before any of us had been hoping to have to fight it.

I cut him off before he could get a full head of steam. "I can handle three enforcers unless they are a whole lot closer than that. Brennan has a rifle, and he can back me up if I need help. You just focus on your quadrant and take your selector off of full auto. We can't afford to waste ammo."

THE DESTROYER

Neither of the two guards I'd just reprimanded looked particularly happy at being dressed down by a girl who was only a few years older than they were, but Brennan nodded.

"She's right, everyone needs to watch their own quadrants and switch to single shot. There's no telling when we'll get a chance to go back for more ammunition. Now let's go into that building that they just left. We need to start spreading the word that people should be moving towards the guard post that sits above that parking garage."

Going through that door was a lot more nerve-racking than I'd been expecting. When I'd assaulted Piter's headquarters, I'd known that anybody I ran into was a bad guy and fair game to shoot, but that wasn't the case here and I couldn't just go through the door at a run. I was working as part of a team this time.

I stopped just outside the door and paused as Brennan stepped up and grabbed the door handle. He waited while I took a deep breath, and then as soon as I nodded, he pulled the door open and I went through, rifle at the ready, finger on the trigger.

There wasn't anybody waiting for us on the ground floor, so Brennan motioned for me to go up the stairs.

We finally found other people on the second floor. They turned and started to run away when they saw us, which was a pretty good sign that they weren't enforcers, but they stopped when Brennan called out to them.

"We aren't here to hurt you. My name is Brennan and I need to talk to someone in charge—this territory is being invaded and everyone needs to get to safety."

I half expected to be forced to wait there for twenty or thirty minutes, but just a few seconds later a burly older man stepped into the hall.

"How do I know you're really who you say you are?"

Brennan chuckled and pointed at his uniform. "Unless you just recently moved into this territory, you recognize the uniform and the guns. I haven't traded enough rifles to other territories yet for anyone else to be fielding five-man teams outside of their own territory. Trust me when I say that I'm the Brennan who runs the compound a few blocks north of here."

The burly man nodded slowly. "Okay, let's say that I believe you. What do you want to talk about?"

"We're under attack right now from all of the territories on our border—"

"I've been living here a long time. Warlords and gang leaders come and go, but the best thing for people like me is just to keep our heads down. One master is much the same as another, the only way life really changes is if someone is stupid enough to stick their head up far enough for it to get chopped off."

Someone like Piter never would've stood for anyone interrupting him like that, but it didn't seem to anger Brennan even as much as it would have Tyrell.

"I get that—believe me, I do. Under normal circumstances, the last thing I would ever do is try to suck people into this fight who don't have a good reason to be risking their lives, but these aren't normal circumstances. Did you look up into the night sky last night, by chance?"

"Yes, what of it?"

"Those lights that you saw tens of thousands of feet above us weren't coming from the ant bombers that we've all gotten used to raining down destruction on us. The ants have parked what they call a mobile command center directly above the city."

"So?"

"So it makes the bombers that we're used to dealing with look like children's toys. They won't use fires to kill us, they'll use metal rods moving at hundreds of miles per hour that are capable of leveling city blocks with each strike."

I expected the building's leader to argue, to protest that what Brennan was describing was impossible, but he didn't. Instead he just bowed his head.

"I always knew this day would come. You can't live in the shadow of a giant for your entire life without coming to understand that someday the giant will crush you like the bug you are.

The only question is why all of you warlords are still squabbling over the crumbs given just how short our time is."

"This doesn't have to be the end. I have good reason to believe that they aren't going to destroy my territory with high-altitude attacks. The shockwaves from the nearby strikes will probably still take down most of these old buildings, but there is an underground structure beneath the southern guard station. If you gather up your people and take them there, I believe that most of you will survive."

The burly guy gave Brennan a calculating look. "They want something from you, don't they? It's the only logical reason for them to spare your territory. You're probably the reason that they decided to attack now."

Brennan opened his mouth, but the other guy had already started moving forward. I acted without thinking, putting a single shot into the floor between his feet.

"The next one will blow a hole in your chest that will let daylight through."

"I don't suppose it makes a difference whether it's you who kills me or the ants. I'll be just as dead either way."

For all of his bravado, he wasn't moving, but that did little to blunt the anger building inside of me. "I personally don't care whether you stay here and die or go to the shelter Brennan's prepared for you, but he does, so I'm out here risking my life in a battle where we're outnumbered thirty or forty to one. You say that you've seen a lot of warlords come through this area—how many of them would have bothered to come looking for you under these circumstances?"

"None of them."

"Yeah, that's what I thought. Now back up before you make me nervous enough to put a bullet into you. Brennan may think that you're worth saving, but I don't trust you enough to let you that close to him."

Brennan shot me a look that said he thought I was coming on too strong, but I didn't lower my rifle until the distance between the two of them was back to what it had been a moment before. Once my rifle came down, Brennan turned back around to the burly building leader.

"What's your name?"

"Hendricks."

"Okay, Hendricks. I've spent as much time here as I can. There are dozens of other buildings that I need to get the word out to, and a battle that I need to go participate in or none of you will have any hope of making it to the guard station. If you believe me, then I need you to send out a group of people to the closest building and let them know what's happening. You have the high ground, you can watch for roaming bands of enforcers and make sure that you only move when the coast is clear.

"We killed a group of enforcers just outside your door. You're welcome to their weapons, but you'll need to be careful not to do anything threatening around any of my guardsmen—I'd hate for your people to get shot. You're going to want to bring as much food and water as you can, and move in groups that are big enough that the enforcers won't mess with you."

Hendricks nodded. "When should we make our move?"

"That will have to be your call. I don't know for sure how things are going to develop between now and tomorrow morning, but you're going to want to have taken cover by the time the sun comes up."

"Okay, we'll do it. I'll have people get word to the surrounding buildings and we'll head out just before sunset. In the meantime, we'll hole up here."

"Sounds good. Be careful of the enforcers. It seems like they've broken up into smaller groups so that they can deny my soldiers easy targets. They are staying off of the streets as much as possible by moving through buildings."

Hendricks' smile was fierce enough to give me chills. "It just might be that we can do something to help out there. We aren't a match for a dozen enforcers—not unarmed and untrained as we are—but if we can get our hands on those weapons and take them by surprise as they come into our building, there's a good chance we can cut them down before they realize what's going on.

"It's nice to be in a situation where we don't have to worry about reprisals for getting a little of our own back against those kinds of monsters. That's always been the biggest reason we've never killed them in droves—at least until recently. Say what they will about you, your people haven't been as bad as the rest of the enforcers we've had come through here."

Brennan stepped forward and shook Hendricks' hand. I didn't like it, but I couldn't order Brennan around. I just kept telling myself that the temporary nanites Tyrell had injected in him would probably be enough to save him from an unarmed civilian—even one as big as Hendricks.

"Anything you can do there would be greatly appreciated, but the most important thing is getting as many of your people out of here in one piece as possible."

A few minutes later we were outside the building again and moving through the streets. Brennan told me to head towards the sound of gunfire, so I did. Half a block from the shooting, we started running into enforcers lurking around the periphery, but they were still in smaller groups so it was fairly easy to bring them down.

All of that changed just before we joined up with the four-man squad the enforcers had pinned down. Whoever was giving the orders on the other side was smart enough to keep the bulk of their guys out of a fight they couldn't win. Instead of rushing soldiers with rifles, they were flanking them with a variety of distance weapons. Everything from bows and arrows to slings and rudimentary blowguns.

I was still in the lead and gunned down a slender guy with a sword and a beefy ax-wielder with quick double taps and then all hell broke loose. We started taking fire—rocks and arrows mostly—almost immediately and I could feel the tension coming off of the new recruits who were supposed to be helping me keep Brennan alive.

We worked our way over to the side of a building whose ground-floor windows had been replaced with metal plates. It meant that we only had a hundred and eighty degrees from which threats could get at us, but I could still tell that the other three soldiers were approaching their breaking point. Most of the incoming fire was relatively unaimed, but that made it only marginally less lethal.

Brennan, on the other hand, was as steady as a rock. He was picking off targets of opportunity in an effort to reduce the hail of projectiles being sent our way.

"There isn't any reason for them to be trying to pin us here like this unless they're moving up additional forces."

I nodded. "Yeah, I suspect they're trying to make sure that we can't meet up with that other squad. If we don't move now we might not get another chance."

"I'll cover you. Take care that you don't get blindsided from inside the building."

A second later Brennan switched to full auto and sent a storm of bullets into the room that seemed to be housing the most accurate set of archers. I took off at a run, adrenaline surging inside of me and my heart hammering away inside of my ribs. I made it ten steps before a flash of movement out of the corner of my eye caused me to throw myself forward. A split second later a three-round burst tore through the space I'd just vacated.

They'd set up one of their few riflemen in a room that had enough of a gap between metal plates for them to be able to take a shot at anybody who ran past, but he'd already ducked back behind cover. I wasn't going to get a shot at him without exposing myself to return fire.

I put my back against the building in an attempt to deny the enemy rifleman a target and then opened up on the building across the way. I hadn't made it far enough to change the angles much, but I managed to bring down an enforcer who popped up to throw a rock at Brennan and the others.

"It's no good, they've got somebody inside the building and the coverage across the windows isn't as complete as it would need to be to deny them shots as you run past."

There was a scream from my left, and for one heart-stopping moment I was worried that they'd hit Brennan. A second later though he called back to me.

"There's more than one inside there. I can hear them moving around behind us. We don't have much time before they're going to rush us, and Crawford just took a bullet to the leg."

I wanted to swear. This wasn't supposed to be such a dangerous fight. The simple fact that we had firearms meant that we could fight ten or fifteen times our number, but the invading territories had brought two or three times that many people and in many ways this was their kind of fight. We didn't have good enough sightlines to really get the full benefit of our superior range. I could only imagine how bad things were going to get once the sun went down.

There was only one way forward. I took off at a run further away from Brennan and the others, headed directly towards the door to the building.

There wasn't time to worry about who might be waiting on the other side of the door when I arrived. Instead of going through like we had back in the last building, I took the door at as close to a run as I could manage. Even that wouldn't have been possible if not for the fact that one of the doors had rusted badly enough that it was propped a quarter of the way open.

I blew through the door, rifle at the ready, and killed a pair of enforcers while they were still trying to react to my sudden appearance. The sound of gunshots inside such a closed area was even more deafening than it had been outside, but temporary deafness was better than the alternative.

I swore as I moved deeper into the building, wishing the whole time that my computer was capable of re-tasking my nanites to deal with the ringing in my ears right away. The nanites would eventually take care of any long-term hearing damage, but that didn't do me much good right then when I desperately needed to hear what was happening around me.

There was a very real risk that I would stumble past somebody and get taken out from behind without ever realizing there was a threat there, but there wasn't anything to be done about it. I just had to keep moving and hope that I could stay ahead of the chaos I was leaving in my wake.

I took a right, headed back in the direction I'd just come from. I hadn't counted windows while I'd been running, so I was going to have to just guess where that shooter had been located.

I only made it half a dozen steps before the first enforcer appeared as if by magic from inside one of the rooms.

I stroked my trigger twice and sent two rounds into his chest in quick succession without slowing down. I approached the room that he'd just left, torn between stopping to make sure it was clear and continuing on to make sure that I made it back to the shooter as quickly as possible.

I was saved from having to decide by the simple fact that that section of the building was even more rusted out than I'd been expecting. I saw movement through one of the holes in the interior wall and sent another bullet tearing into the flesh of the remaining enforcer in the room.

I was still moving fast, as close to a dead run as I could manage and still have a chance of hitting a moving target, but it wasn't fast enough to outrun the sound of my shots. The next door that opened did so right as I came even with it. I slammed the butt of my rifle into the head of a tall guy with half a dozen facial piercings, and then pivoted to blow a hole through the chest of a shaven-headed white guy with crude tattoos covering his right arm.

The bolt on my rifle locked back as I was trying to traverse its muzzle towards the last remaining threat. I had a split second to realize just how much trouble I was in and then a beefy black guy charged me, leading the way with a knife that was almost as long as my arm.

My options were limited. He was coming from my left, which meant that my rifle was out of position if I wanted to club him like I had the first guy from the room, and based on how quickly he was moving and how heavy he was, there wasn't anything I could do to stop him before he crashed into me. Supercharged muscles and nanite-infused bones were an incredible equalizer, but there was still only so much they could do to offset the laws of physics.

I slapped my right hand against his forearm and then set the butt of my rifle against the doorframe I'd just stepped through. I wasn't strong enough to stop him head on, but I did manage to stabilize the rifle enough with one hand that when he crashed into it the barrel was driven deep into his chest.

His knife still sliced a hot, painful line across my back, but my rifle's barrel stood up to the abuse I'd just inflicted on it. The collision robbed him of most of his momentum, but the impact still knocked me back into the doorframe hard enough that I half expected to hear my ribs crack.

I had, however, managed to keep my chin tucked enough that my head didn't slam into the unyielding metal, and that meant I wasn't disoriented. As I bounced off of the doorframe, I hammered my right foot into his knee, shattering the joint and sending him towards the ground. I ripped my rifle free of his body as he started to fall and then thrust the butt into his head with enough force to snap his neck.

I ejected my spent magazine and slammed a fresh one home as I staggered back out into the corridor. There wasn't time to inspect the barrel, I had to just trust in the manufacturing quality of the weapon I'd been given. I aimed the barrel deeper into the building and squeezed off a single shot hoping the rifle wasn't about to explode in my hands.

It didn't, which meant my only other worry was that the sights had been thrown out of alignment or the barrel had been bent from the collision. Before I could bring the rifle back up to my shoulder and squeeze off another shot—this one aimed—another figure stepped out into the hallway.

He was good, and he wasn't just armed with the same primitive weaponry as nearly everyone else I'd run into so far. This guy had one of Brennan's rifles, and unlike me, it was snugged up against his shoulder and the barrel was already tracking towards me.

My thumb flipped the selector over to full auto, and I held the trigger down without even trying to aim. Under normal circumstances the recoil from bullets exiting the barrel at something better than the speed of sound was something I had to fight. Even the heavy, all-metal rifles turned out in the compound required a significant amount of effort if you wanted to fight barrel rise.

This time I didn't even try to fight it. Instead, I tracked my shots to the left and let recoil stitch a line of crimson across my enemy from hip to shoulder. The enforcer went down in a spray of blood as I ricocheted off the wall and continued stumbling forward.

THE DESTROYER

I checked the room my latest victim had just left and confirmed that it was empty. "Brennan, I just eliminated the shooter. You guys are good to move, I'll meet you at the door."

"We're on our way!"

I headed back out of the room, stopping to grab the rifle and single spare magazine that the enforcer had been carrying. I didn't expect to get any use out of it unless my rifle really had been warped, but there was no reason to leave it behind for somebody else to use against us. Besides, I was nearly out of ammunition.

My return trip back to the door was uneventful right up until I entered the foyer. Three guys with bows shot arrows at me at the same time, and it was all I could do to get back around the corner without being hit.

I took a deep breath and then sprang around the corner, rifle firing as soon as I had a target. My first shot took the archer on the left through the chest as a trio of arrows streaked through the space where I'd been standing just a split second before. I was still so hopped up on adrenaline that it almost seemed like the arrows were visible as they flashed past, but I didn't let that slow me down. A good archer was capable of firing incredibly quickly and if I didn't manage to bring the other two down then Brennan and the others would be walking into a trap.

The second archer went down right as he got his next arrow into the air. I took him with a single shot to the head a split second before an arrow took me through the leg. There was nothing structurally wrong with my limb at that point, but the shock and pain made it buckle despite my best efforts.

I flipped the selector on my rifle back to full auto and squeezed off another long burst as I fell, blowing multiple holes in the last archer's chest. My left knee hit the ground at the same time the archer did, and the pain from that impact was every bit as bad as the red-hot awl of pain where the arrow had lodged in my leg. I forced myself back up to my feet despite the throbbing in my left knee and turned just in time to see Brennan throw open one of the doors.

Everything happened in slow motion. I had plenty of time to look past Brennan and see another shooter step into view across the street. I hadn't realized that the enforcers we were up against were ruthless enough to sacrifice so many of their number, to let me past without a shot just so that they would have a better chance to take out the bulk of our group. I'd severely underestimated them.

The enforcer across the street was only marginally skilled with his weapon, but he had the bulk required to steady it, and the range was so short that almost anyone could have had their target. He opened up on full auto and geysers of blood erupted from both the guard who was supposed to be covering Brennan's retreat and his partner who'd been dragging our wounded squad member towards safety.

They were both dead, even if they hadn't realized it yet. They each had multiple exit wounds that I wasn't sure even nanites could have stabilized. There wasn't anything I could do to save them, but that didn't mean I couldn't avenge them.

I squeezed off a trio of quick shots in an attempt to force the shooter back under cover, and then probably would've run to grab the one soldier who still had a chance of surviving if not for the grunt I heard from Brennan a split second later. I turned to find that he'd been shot by a fourth archer who was already drawing his bowstring back for another shot.

I threw myself into Brennan, knocking him out of the path of the arrow, and hissed as it nicked my left arm. Brennan hit the ground harder than I'd expected, but there wasn't time to stop and check his injuries.

I spun back around the corner and fired off my last remaining bullet from the set of magazines I'd brought with me from the compound. I hadn't been counting my shots—and therefore hadn't realized how low that magazine was getting—so I'd been expecting to be able to make a second attempt.

I'd rushed the shot, and was lucky I managed to hit him at all. I took him in the leg and had the satisfaction of seeing him hit the ground as I ducked back behind cover.

I had only seconds before more enforcers were going to show up on the scene. We'd killed many times our number, but whoever was in charge on the other side was spending his men like water in an attempt to bring us down. This wasn't going to be about who had the most men when the dust settled. It was going to be about which of our enemies managed to arrive at the compound first with enough men to hold it against the rest of the warlords and gang leaders who were gunning for us. Whoever was coming at us from the south was obviously banking on being able to get ammunition for whatever guns he captured once he got to the compound.

I checked Brennan over. He'd taken an arrow to the gut, down low on the left side. Fortunately, I didn't think it had hit his kidney. It was still going to be touch and go, but I was hoping that meant his nanites—whatever was left over from the last injection Tyrell had given him—would be able to save him. Assuming I was able to get him away from ten or twenty times our number of experienced, bloodthirsty enforcers.

A couple of widely spaced shots came zipping through the open doors, fired more to keep our heads down than because the shooter had any expectation of hitting us. That was a bad sign, because it meant that the shooter knew he just needed to keep us pinned down until his reinforcements could get close enough to rush us.

I grabbed Brennan's arm and pulled him up to his feet. He helped, but not as much as I'd been hoping.

"Can you walk?"

"Yeah, for a little ways at least. How much ammunition do you have left?"

I shook my head. We were past the point where the number of bullets left in our guns was going to make a difference. I still had the spare magazine from the enforcer who'd tried to shoot me as I ran past on the street, but even if I managed to kill an enforcer with each of my remaining bullets, all that was going to do was tell the dozen or so remaining bad guys exactly where we were.

I suddenly realized what I was going to have to do. I grabbed Brennan and half carried him back in the direction I'd just come from.

None of the people I'd killed back in that direction were a good match for me, but the shooter had actually been not that far off of Brennan's build and coloring. I reached over to Brennan's vest and started undoing buckles as we walked. It wasn't easy with one hand, but once he figured out what I was doing he helped out—grabbing a spare magazine and a couple of other items out of his pockets as he stripped out of it.

Once we arrived at the shooter, I lifted him up to a sitting position and slipped Brennan's vest onto him. The shirt underneath the vest wasn't a very close match to the standard uniform Jax had designed, but I had a sneaking suspicion that the enforcers weren't going to be looking at the bodies very closely. They were after the rifles and their minds would fill in the details they were expecting to see.

I buckled the fasteners across the front of the vest, rolled the dead enforcer back over onto his stomach so that he was closer to the guy I'd stabbed with my rifle, and then grabbed the big knife that had come so close to skewering me and shoved it into the enforcer I'd just finished dressing up.

It had all turned out better than I'd been expecting. The vest even hid the exit wounds out of the enforcer's back. I dropped my empty gun to the floor and then used the gun I'd captured to fire off a couple of shots in random directions. With any luck I figured that would explain the other bodies and keep people's heads down for a few more seconds.

Brennan was leaning against the wall like it was the only thing keeping him standing, but he pushed away from it as I reached him, and he was walking better than he had been a few moments before. Either he was starting to get over some of the shock of being wounded, or his borrowed nanites were starting to address the worst of the damage.

"Where are we headed?"

THE DESTROYER

I shouldn't have been able to hear Brennan—not after being exposed to so much sustained gunfire—but I could. It was a good thing, too—we couldn't afford to have anyone overhear us yelling to each other.

"Upstairs, if we can find the stairwell. It's the last place they would expect us to go."

"Yeah, on account of the fact that we'll be trapped up there. I hope your plan works."

I projected a confidence I didn't feel. "It will. We just need to get far enough ahead to make sure that we aren't leaving a blood trail."

"By we, you mean me. Your bleeding has already nearly stopped and it never got bad enough to fill up your boots."

We kept moving as we talked, and I realized he was right. He was leaving behind bloody footsteps every time his right foot touched the ground, but I wasn't. That was good—my plan relied on the bad guys having kept score of how many of us there were left and the entire plan would have fallen to pieces if they'd noticed two sets of bloody footprints headed away from the scene I'd just staged.

We found a set of stairs and started upwards as I heard people enter the building. The tension inside of me ratcheted up even higher as I realized just how many things could still go wrong in the next few minutes. Adrenaline was still surging through my system, but that wasn't doing anything to stop the sweat pooling between my shoulder blades. It was a good thing that I'd brought Lexis' hat with me—it caught the perspiration that otherwise would have been blinding me.

We hit the top of the first flight of stairs and I motioned Brennan to continue on to the third floor. Once we arrived there I led him out of the stairwell and helped him down to a sitting position. I could hear people moving around below us, but it sounded like we still had a little bit of time before they finished checking the first floor.

I pulled off my vest as Brennan slid down the wall with a groan. It took me only a moment to empty my pockets and slip the things that had been in my vest into one of the pockets in my cargo pants.

I then pulled out the knife that I carried in my right boot and used it to cut a strip of fabric off of the bottom of my shirt. I spent a few seconds examining Brennan's wound and then cut his shirt away from the arrow in his side.

"It's no good. Hold still while I cut the rest of your shirt off of you."

"Don't cut the entire thing away. I'll freeze up here without a shirt once the sun goes down. Just cut enough so you can get at the arrow."

I shook my head as I continued to slit the seam running up his side. "We don't have a choice. You're going to need something to wrap around your shoe if we're going to avoid leaving a blood trail, and this is as much of my shirt as I'm cutting off. We don't have much time—you're going to have to deal with your shoe while I deal with the arrow."

The pain in my leg—both my knee and the arrow still lodged in my flesh—was even worse now that I was kneeling in front of Brennan, but I just gritted my teeth and forced myself to proceed. I used my knife to score the shaft of the arrow in Brennan's side and then broke it with one quick jerk.

He hissed in pain, but managed to avoid making enough noise to lead any of our enemies directly to us. I sheathed my knife, slid the rest of the arrow out of his side and then set about binding the holes while he tied the rest of his shirt around his left shoe. The whole process took less than thirty seconds and then I was helping him back to his feet.

"There should be another set of stairs in every corner of the building. I need you to run to the closest set. I'll be right behind you."

I could see the questions in Brennan's eyes, but he didn't voice them. He just nodded and used the wall to pull himself back up to his feet.

"I've got a limited amount of time before the blood leaks through my shirt and we're back to having the same problem."

"I know. When you get to the stairs go up to the next floor."

I gave him a little push to get him started, waited twenty seconds and then turned and blindly fired a single shot down into the stairwell, being careful to keep a wall between me and the muzzle of my gun in the hopes it would muffle the sound. The ringing was back, but it wasn't as bad as before. I could hear people running around below us. The only question was how many of them would choose to come up these stairs versus how many would go up one of the other sets.

I could already tell that they weren't performing any kind of organized search. They were each too worried about being the one to find us and get a rifle to worry about whether or not I was herding them.

I turned, scooped up my vest, and ran, catching up with Brennan just after he made it to the stairwell at the other end of the building. I motioned for him to keep going and then started looking for a good hiding place.

I could hear people moving around in the building, some below and some on my level, but it didn't sound like anyone was coming up this particular stairwell. That was probably good, assuming I could find a decent place to set up my ambush.

Heart pounding, I examined the closest three rooms. The first two were no good—too many holes in the wall or bad access to the hallway—but the third seemed like it might work. I let my stolen rifle hang freely on its sling and pulled my knife back out of the sheath in my boot. This wasn't going to work if I made a bunch of noise.

It was the kind of crazy plan my instructors back home would never have approved of. There were too many variables that I couldn't control. If I couldn't lure a small enough group into range, or if there were other groups besides my target group who were close enough to realize what I was doing, then I was a dead woman.

That would've made what I was trying to do plenty risky enough, but when you threw in the fact that I was about to go up against hardened, experienced killers with nothing more than a knife—their weapon of choice—I was basically signing my own death warrant.

On the plus side, if I died down there on the third floor, there was still a good chance that none of the enforcers would ever realize that Brennan was still alive up on the fourth floor.

I could hear several sets of footsteps getting closer. It was hard to tell—they were moving irregularly—but it sounded to me like three enforcers. That was right on the edge of what I was capable of in my wildest dreams. Taking one enforcer out in a surprise attack would be child's play. A second enforcer would make things much more complicated, but was still doable with a little bit of luck. That was all well and good, but I was having a hard time imagining a situation where I could take the second enforcer out before the third enforcer gutted me.

It was tempting to just wait. It was always possible that another group—of only two people—would pass by a few minutes after this first group. The enforcers seem to be using irregularly sized squads, but I knew in my gut that would be a mistake. Once this first squad ran into another group they would turn around and head straight back here with the intent of going upstairs and searching the next floor. If I let that happen, then Brennan's odds of survival went down dramatically.

I strained my battered hearing in an attempt to determine if anyone else was close enough to interfere, but my ears simply weren't up to the task. I took a deep breath while the approaching squad was still half a dozen yards away and then held it as they got closer. I'd positioned myself in the deepest shadow available in the room, but that still wasn't any guarantee. If they had any kind of portable light then I was going to stick out like a sore thumb.

I could hear them checking the first two rooms that I'd considered using for my ambush. It sounded like they were checking multiple rooms simultaneously, which gave me the first glimmer of hope that I might actually survive what was about to happen.

A few seconds later a short guy stepped halfway into my room and did a quick visual inspection. It was difficult to tell in the dim lighting, but it almost seemed like his eyes lingered on my corner for a heartbeat longer than the rest of the room. I felt like my pulse was loud enough for him to hear from across the hall, but after only a second or two he turned to leave.

It was the best opportunity I was going to get. I shot forward like a striking rattlesnake. My knife took him in the kidney as I stabbed and then sliced outward with my right hand while my left cupped his mouth in an effort to stop him from yelling.

The wash of blood from his severed renal artery would've made me sick under other circumstances, but I was so terrified he was going to alert his friends that there wasn't space inside of my mind to think about anything other than surviving. I pulled him backwards, keeping him off balance as I waited for all the blood he was losing to catch up with him.

I was desperately trying to remember what I'd learned from my instructors, but I couldn't remember if it was twenty seconds to unconsciousness and forty seconds to death, or forty seconds to unconsciousness and sixty seconds to death. Either way, it was taking much too long. I could already hear one of the enforcer's companions headed back my direction.

"Toss, stop screwing around and get out here. You may not care about getting to spend time with the girls, but I want one of those rifles, and I'm not going to let you ruin this for me."

I was running out of time and I knew it. I'd pulled my victim back far enough into the room that we were effectively invisible, but that didn't do anything to conceal the trail of blood that started just inside the door. It wasn't glaringly obvious—I'd started pulling the enforcer backwards before his clothes had soaked all the way through—but it was definitely there, and based on the way the second enforcer had slowed down, he was suspicious enough to notice it unless I acted soon.

I pushed the enforcer I'd stabbed across the room with enough force that I figured he had a reasonable chance of hitting the far wall. I misjudged his weight—that or just how far he was gone. He only made it six feet before collapsing to the floor, but as soon as he hit the ground I exploded around the corner.

I'd been hoping that the crash would confuse my next target as to where the real threat was located, but I'd known it was a long shot. The second enforcer stepped backwards as I came into view. He was desperately trying to buy himself enough space to get his sword—a huge two-handed monstrosity that was almost comical in the grip of someone only an inch taller than me—into play, but for once I wasn't lacking commitment to my attack. I'd known that my only chance rested in getting to within a foot or two so I could employ the bloody knife in my right hand.

THE DESTROYER

I had youth and cutting-edge technology on my side, but he was just as desperate as me, and he had more than a decade of experience in these kinds of situations to draw on. I'd been expecting him to continue to try to get his sword into play. Instead he lashed out with a kick that was no less effective for all that it was ugly and lacking in any definable technique.

It was the kind of thing no martial artist from inside the Society military would've considered using, but it was exactly the kind of thing I should've expected out of someone who was only half a step up from a bar-room brawler. I tried to get far enough to the side to dodge the kick, but even my nanites couldn't give me enough of an edge to accomplish that.

The blow clipped me on my left hip, turning me slightly as it knocked me backwards, so I did the only thing I could. I stabbed my knife into his calf and used it for leverage to stop myself from being knocked to the ground. The enforcer went white from the pain involved in receiving an eight-inch-long cut, but that didn't stop him from continuing to bring his sword around.

I was completely out of position for the attack I'd been intending on using, and even if that hadn't been the case, there was no way I could block a blow from such a heavy weapon with nothing more than a combat knife, so I didn't even try. I left my knife embedded in his calf and whipped my rifle up so that the blow from his sword slammed into the heavy, metal shoulder stock.

It was like being kicked by a rhinoceros. The force of the blow slammed me back into the wall behind me with enough force to crack one of my ribs, but I somehow managed to hold onto my rifle, and that saved me from being cut in half.

As the huge, two-handed sword ricocheted away from me, it was incredibly tempting to just shoot the enforcer before he could recover, but I knew I couldn't do that. Any thought of trying to keep the confrontation quiet enough not to alert the third enforcer, whom I could hear coming back out of a room further down the hall, had gone by the wayside when I'd slammed into the side of the corridor hard enough to make the metal ring, but I still couldn't take the easy way out. This guy was the closest thing I was going to get to a good physical match to me, which meant that I needed him to die from something other than a gunshot wound.

I just needed it to happen within the next second or two before his friend joined in the fight.

The force of the blow I'd just blocked had staggered me, but apparently I'd managed to surprise my opponent. Under other circumstances there wouldn't have been any way for me to have blocked such a powerful swing. My bones and muscles would've been up to the task, but someone as light as I was simply didn't have enough mass to avoid getting knocked over. Getting thrown into the wall had hurt, but it had turned things into a contest solely of strength rather than strength and size.

I'd been able to lock my elbows and withstand his blow, which had sent the sword whipping back away towards the other wall at a clip that had obviously surprised my opponent. I took advantage of that shock to throw myself forward and landed a solid blow to his ribs with the butt of my rifle.

The sound of breaking bone was one of the most welcome things I'd ever heard. I hadn't killed him—not given how far down on his chest I'd landed the blow—but I was pretty sure he wasn't going to manage to generate the same kind of power as he had with his first strike. It was a risk, but rather than trying to finish him off I spun around and blew out the back of the third enforcer's head with a single round from my much-abused rifle.

A whisper of sound was the only warning I received, but it was still just enough to bring me around in time to interpose my rifle between me and that damn sword. The weapon was so heavy that it still packed quite the kinetic energy, but it was nothing like what I'd been up against the first time he'd hit me. Not only did I manage to keep my feet under me, I rotated my hips and slammed an elbow into his throat before he could recover from his latest swing.

He was gagging and choking, and I knew it was only a matter of time before he would suffocate, but I couldn't just leave him there to let nature take its course. I grabbed his right arm to make sure I had control of his sword, and pulled him back towards the room where I'd killed the first enforcer.

I slammed his arm against the wall, causing him to drop his sword, and then dropped him to the ground and tore my knife free from his leg and cut his throat. It wasn't the way I would've chosen to treat a vanquished enemy, but I needed to make sure that it was obvious he died from something other than rifle fire.

My hands were shaking as I slipped my vest on him and then grabbed my hat and used it to cover his face. I slid his sword into a dark corner of the nearby room, and then dropped my captured rifle as I picked up my knife and ran towards the stairs. I could hear people closing in on me from nearly every direction. I had mere seconds before they would arrive. The only question now was whether anyone was close enough to see me before I made it up the stairs.

Chapter 5

I did manage to make it to the top of the stairs just in the nick of time to avoid being seen by the enforcers, but I couldn't be sure of that for several minutes. I ended up sitting there on the fourth floor just outside the stairwell for nearly five minutes with my heart pounding the entire time while I waited to see if the enforcers would see through my deception.

I would've liked to have worked my way deeper inside the fourth floor in the hopes of being hard to find, but I was close enough to hear them talking. That meant that I was close enough for them to hear me if I started moving around and accidentally stumbled over some bit of garbage, so I was forced to listen as the enforcers argued over who was going to get to carry the rifle back to their boss.

Whatever tiny portion of my brain remained unmonopolized by my worries about the enforcers was focused on Brennan. I hadn't thought to tell him where to wait for me. It was entirely possible that he was somewhere on the fourth floor wondering if I'd survived my last encounter with our enemies, but there was no guarantee of that. It was equally likely that he'd chosen to go up another flight or two of stairs before going to ground.

At least I knew he still had a rifle and enough rounds to deal with anyone who happened to stumble on to him. It would still mean that we would both end up dead, but I knew he would feel better selling himself dearly if it came to that.

As the enforcers started to move out I realized that I'd missed my best opportunity to remove the arrow from my leg. Once I'd heard them arguing about who was going to get the rifle I should've gone ahead and cut the projectile free of my flesh. Now that they were moving around, and potentially headed my direction, it was too dangerous to try doctoring myself. If they hadn't bought into the narrative I'd set up for them, I'd end up being forced to run away from them with blood pouring out of the twin holes left in my leg after extracting the arrow.

Actually, the more I thought about it, the more I realized how incredible it was that I hadn't pulled it out as soon as I made it up to the fourth floor. I'd been injured often enough in training to know that, under the right circumstances, pain could become enough of a constant that you were able to move past it, but this was something else. The pain that had been almost debilitating just a few minutes ago had somehow morphed into nothing more than a dull ache. I would've worried that I was suffering from some kind of nerve damage, but I could still clearly feel my toes squishing around inside my left boot.

The enforcers seemed to be heading downstairs, but they were making so much racket I couldn't be sure. It was hard to envision a situation where they would've felt like I was enough of a threat to make a big production of half of them heading downstairs while the other half snuck up to the fourth floor in an attempt to take me unawares, but that didn't stop a new surge of adrenaline from shooting through my body.

Even after the ruckus finally died away I still didn't dare move until Brennan found me more than ten minutes later.

"Skye, are you okay?"

He was whispering, but I still had to fight the urge to order him to stop talking. The odds were good that we were by ourselves now, but even if we weren't I needed to get myself bandaged up. With my nanites going all-out trying to repair the damage to my body, the longer I waited before extracting the arrow, the more damage it would end up doing to the wound when I pulled it out.

"I think so. Let's move back so we are less exposed and then I need to get this out of my leg."

Brennan nodded and then helped me to my feet. He wasn't a whole lot steadier than I was, and had the added challenge of carrying around a rifle to boot, but I appreciated the attempt. I wasn't positive I could've made it back up to my feet all by myself.

"I found a room back this way with windows that are boarded up enough that we shouldn't be seen, but not so much as to make it too dark to operate on you. I tried not to move around a ton, but I figured there was a pretty good chance that they would attribute any noise I made up here to rats."

I opened my mouth in shock, unable to believe that I'd been so stupid. He was absolutely right. Despite my time in the city, I still thought like someone raised on the other side of the barrier. Then again, maybe that wasn't entirely fair. I hadn't actually spent that much time outside the compound, and Brennan's rigorous rules meant that the compound hadn't been nearly as infested with vermin as the rest of the city.

I was half tempted to get angry at myself for making such a big mistake, but I ended up just chuckling. "I guess I should've been walking around looking for you this entire time. I never even considered that they might blame any noise I made on anything other than me."

The room Brennan led me to was everything I could've asked for—considering the fact that I was in a dirty, decaying building that hadn't had running water or heat for a century and a half. At least it was relatively free of garbage, and the light was just as good as Brennan had indicated it would be.

I seated myself in the best pool of light I could find and then wiped my knife on my pants.

"I guess it's kind of silly to be worried about cleaning this thing off before I try to cut a dirty arrow out of my leg. My nanites should be able to take care of any kind of foreign organism that tries to use me as a host—it just feels kind of weird to stick something dripping with somebody else's blood inside of me."

Brennan shrugged. "I don't know, that sounds like a pretty healthy instinct. You can't have had your nanites for very long. Before you became a franchised citizen I suspect that kind of thing was just as important for you as it is for those of us on this side of the barrier."

I nodded absently as I cut a groove around the arrow still lodged in my leg. I snapped the shaft off cleanly and then realized I needed something to serve as a bandage before I went any further. I resignedly sacrificed another strip of fabric off of the bottom of my shirt and then nodded for Brennan to rip the arrow out of my leg.

It wasn't until I was in the middle of tying my improvised binding around my leg that I realized what it was about his comment that had seemed so off to me.

"How is it that you know so much about Society life? I kept thinking that it was just another thing that Tyrell had taught you, but that doesn't make sense either. He hasn't been on the other side of the barrier for a hundred and fifty years. Heck, the last time he was there, the barrier hadn't even been built yet."

"Actually, that's not quite true. The barrier was operational before Alexander tried to kill him. From what I understand, the enclave where Tyrell and Alexander did most of their work was the most top-of-the-line research facility in the entire world. They pretty much had everything you can think of there. A self-contained power grid, its own water supply, greenhouses capable of feeding the entire population of the facility, and an energy barrier capable of shrugging off anything up to and including a small nuclear warhead."

I shook my head in amazement. "Even after all this time, after everything you and Tyrell have told me, I'm still having a hard time realizing just how much of our history is nothing more than lies. What about the manufacturing facilities?"

Brennan shrugged. "That's not something that's ever come up between Tyrell and me, but it wouldn't surprise me to find out that there were some kind of light manufacturing facilities there before the Desolation. The entire point of the facility was to make it so that they didn't have to lower the barrier very often."

THE DESTROYER

"Because every time the barrier went down there was a chance that someone would try to get in and sabotage the work they were doing there."

"Yeah, that's pretty much the size of it. There were hundreds—maybe even thousands—of people living inside what amounted to a gigantic, indestructible bubble just so that the multibillionaires who owned the facility could make sure that the scientists at the top of the food chain could continue their work uninterrupted. Once Tyrell signed up to do his research at that location, he pretty much knew that the only way he was ever going to be able to leave would be if he managed to find a way to make nanites economical enough for everyone in the world to have them."

"I guess there's one situation where you're better off not being the best and the brightest."

"You would think, but that wasn't really the case. All of the normal people who were responsible for growing the food or keeping the machinery running were even less able to leave. They got paid well enough that most of them didn't actually want out, but from what I understand, it was all but impossible for even them to leave."

I racked my brain for what little history I'd been taught about the time before the Desolation. It had all been so long ago that I was having a hard time remembering what I'd been told.

"I thought that wasn't legal. I mean, it's not like I can believe what I was taught in grade school—not after all the things they lied to me about—but I always understood that the pre-Desolation governments were big on individual liberty."

Brennan nodded. "Yeah, for the most part. There were exceptions, places that ironically were a lot more like the Society that Alexander has created behind the barrier now, but most of the cultures in the West had a high degree of freedom. The enclave's owners claimed to have a procedure in place for those citizens who wanted to leave the facility, but Tyrell said that it was so involved that almost no one ever made it out. Given all of that, it only makes sense that they must have been manufacturing the bulk of what they needed there inside of the enclave."

"So it was all basically a lie. Everything we have—they have—on the other side of the barrier wasn't created by their ancestors as a result of some kind of superior social system, it was built by the same unimaginably rich capitalists that the precepts vilify."

"Yeah, that's about the shape of it. A lot of the automation probably came later on, but there's simply no way Alexander could've built up the technology base he has with a group of people who work, on average, less than two hours a week."

"I guess that makes sense. I saw how hard everyone was working in the compound. I should've realized that, even with all of our fancy technology, we still couldn't have gotten to where we are with such little ongoing effort."

I scooted over closer to the hole that had once upon a time housed a window. "As fascinating as this has been, you haven't answered my question. How do you guys know all of this given that neither of you have been inside the barrier during the last century and a half?"

"You remember us talking about Katya?"

"Yes, I take it that she's your spy?"

"That's right, but she's more than just a spy, she is the reason that Tyrell and I were able to come to this city. I wasn't born here."

"I didn't even know that was possible. I thought that the Society's military had managed to completely shut down movement between cities."

"They have—for anyone who doesn't happen to have one of your planes. That's the thing about Katya, she isn't one of us pretending to be one of you, she's one of you who's defected over to our side."

I rocked backwards, shaking my head in amazement. "The Citizen-President was lying about that too, wasn't he? He told me we'd never sent an actual operative in to infiltrate one of the cities before me, but that wasn't the case."

"Yeah, I'm afraid not. It's actually part of Alexander's standard operating procedure. He knows that he can't depend on his people to innovate, so he uses micro drones to maintain surveillance on anyone he thinks has a chance of coming up with something new. Once he identifies someone with something he wants, he injects an operative with an unlocked version of his nanites and then sends them into the city to steal it from the real owner. It's such an effective ploy precisely because Alexander has convinced the entire world that the ants only perform long-distance surveillance."

Even in just the short time that we'd been talking, the sun had already made surprising progress in its journey towards the horizon. The shadows inside our room were getting longer and longer, and the temperature was starting to drop. I rubbed my arms, conscious of just how much skin was showing around my midsection now that the air had a chill to it, as I considered Brennan's words.

"How did it happen? How did you and Tyrell meet up with Katya?"

Brennan was even colder than I was given that he had so much more bare skin exposed to the elements, but as he moved closer to me and shyly wrapped an arm around my shoulders, I got the feeling he was more concerned about my discomfort than he was about his own growing chill.

"This all happened before my time, so it was just Tyrell—Tyrell and Jax—but the story starts out about like you'd expect. Tyrell had started trying to reestablish a decent technology base in one of the cities five or six hundred miles south of here. His progress was painfully slow, since steam-era technology isn't exactly his area of expertise, but he was making progress."

I leaned further into Brennan, welcoming his body heat at the same time that my heart started racing simply because this was the closest we'd ever been to each other.

"Wasn't he worried about Alexander realizing it was him behind the progress?"

"Sort of. Alexander came within a hair's breadth of killing Tyrell back before he kicked off the Desolation, and Tyrell managed to keep a very low profile between then and whenever he snuck out of the enclave. There was no guarantee that Alexander was still convinced that he'd succeeded in killing Tyrell, but it had been more than a hundred years since Tyrell had picked up anything indicating that the ants were after him specifically. He figured if he changed his face there was a chance he could get things started back up inside of one city and then use it as a jumping-off point in a war against Alexander."

"That seems like an awfully big gamble given just how powerful of a military Alexander had assembled."

Brennan shrugged gingerly, obviously trying to avoid pulling at the wound in his side. "Yes and no. I'm not sure I could've done that if it had been me in Tyrell's shoes, but it had been a long time. Tyrell had kept his head down for something like a hundred and thirty years. Back then the Society didn't have travel between the cities completely choked out and Tyrell had watched Alexander bomb city after city into something only slightly better than a mass grave yard. Things weren't always like this. Even eighty or ninety years ago there were entire cities, or at least pockets inside of some cities, where technology hadn't completely been destroyed."

I slipped my left arm around behind Brennan's back and edged my hips closer to his, thrilling slightly when I felt the side of my leg make contact with his.

"I suspect it's not going to surprise you if I say that inside of the Society we are taught that every city in the world had been reduced to something only barely above subsistence level within a decade or two of the Desolation."

"No, not at all. Alexander would've liked to have done that shortly after he took over the enclave, but he knew he needed isolated pockets where real progress was still taking place. It was the only way he was going to have any chance of stealing the technologies he needed to further cement his control over your people.

"That was part of why Tyrell thought that he might be able to get away with starting a technological Renaissance. By that point, the ants had knocked everybody so far backwards that there wasn't any chance of truly useful technology being developed on this side of the barrier. Tyrell figured that Alexander would be eager for someone to start regaining ground so that his people would be able to swoop back in and steal anything useful."

One of the many pieces of the official history suddenly clicked into place with what Brennan was telling me. "That was before we built the mobile command centers, wasn't it?"

"Bingo. That's the other reason that Tyrell felt like his plan had a chance of succeeding. Even back then, the population growth inside the barrier was flirting with negative numbers, and all indications were that Alexander was keeping travel suppressed between the various cities by only the very thinnest of margins."

I nodded, mind racing as I continued to put disparate pieces of the puzzle together. "So Tyrell started an industrial revolution, but Alexander never really believed that he'd died back before the Desolation, which is why he sent in Katya."

"It's hard to say. Her mission was different than yours. Rather than stealing technology like all the operatives who'd come before her, she was supposed to find and eliminate Tyrell, which could mean that Alexander did indeed suspect that there was more to the role Tyrell was playing than met the eye."

"So what happened? Did Tyrell know what Alexander was going to attempt?"

"She fell in love. Nobody expected it, not her, not Tyrell, and not Alexander, but that's what happened."

"In love with who, or what?"

I was almost positive it was a who rather than a what, but the parallels between Katya's situation and mine were uncomfortable enough that I didn't want to just assume she'd betrayed her Society for a guy.

"I guess when you come right down to it, it was both. Even back then, the Society was the kind of place where people didn't do anything but feed their addictions. I think seeing all of the energy inside of the city, all the progress that Tyrell was responsible for, was eye-opening for her in a way that she wasn't ready for. That probably wouldn't have been enough though all by itself to make her abandon her mission, but there was also a who—more than one who, actually."

"Like polygamy?"

Brennan chuckled. "Careful, you'll ruin my perception of the ants as being world-weary parasites for whom nothing is forbidden."

I was blushing as I punched him in the leg. "Your perceptions are all wrong. The truth is that everything is forbidden, most of us just don't pay attention to the rules. They call it the social desirability index. Marriage is good, work is good, service to your fellow man is good. Those things all create the proper bonds inside of the Society to allow it to continue forward. Addictive drugs, casual sex, and multi-partner pairings on the other hand are considered to be inherently unstable and therefore detrimental to society."

"I've never heard it explained in quite those terms, but I guess I shouldn't be surprised. I always thought that there really weren't any rules inside the barrier, but it makes a lot more sense to come at it from the direction that Alexander has. If you want children to behave in a particular way, the quickest solution is to tell them that those particular behaviors are prohibited."

"Wait, are you saying that Alexander actually wants people to do all those things?"

"Absolutely. That's how he makes sure that he always has control over the enclave. If people were ever to stop doing what they were supposed to, he would just shut down their access to whatever it was they are addicted to. That's doubly the case for the military. There are probably a few decent eggs even there, but the vast bulk of Alexander's trained killers signed up for that duty precisely because the military is given access to ways of satisfying darker addictions than even what the general populace enjoys."

The chill that crawled through me wasn't just because of the rapidly dropping temperatures around us. It was the result of a realization as to what had happened the one and only time I'd left the approved areas inside the enclave.

The man who'd attempted to force me hadn't just been a random citizen, he'd been part of the military. Even more astonishing, the woman who'd saved me had understood exactly what was going on. That implied an understanding of the true nature of the Society on the part of at least some of the franchised citizens that vastly exceeded my own during the time when I'd been back home. I wasn't just the victim of a massive cover-up. I was less observant than I should've been.

Brennan seemed to have sensed that something had changed for me. He turned in an attempt to meet my eyes.

"Are you okay, Skye?"

I wasn't sure what to tell him. Knowing that the military recruits I'd been training with were just as bad as the guy who'd tried to rape me, was throwing me for a loop. I hadn't been particularly close to any of them, but it still made my skin crawl to think that I'd spent so much time with them and dozens of other military personnel without ever suspecting the truth.

I wasn't sure I dared tell Brennan just how blind I'd been, not now that I realized there were others from the Society who hadn't been as blind to what was going on as I'd been.

I cleared my throat and nodded. "Yeah, I'm just still trying to reconcile what I was taught with the truth. You were saying that Katya fell in love?"

"Yes, with two people—although in very different ways. One of Tyrell's people had just given birth to a baby girl shortly before Katya arrived, and part of the cover she chose required extensive interaction between her, the baby, and the baby's mother. That awakened a maternal instinct inside of her that I'm not sure anyone could've predicted."

"I don't understand, how did a baby make her want to defect?"

"It wasn't just the baby, it was Jax too. Katya fell in love with Jax and the idea of being a mother at the same time and it opened up a whole new world of possibilities for her. She saw a future where she could be proud of having helped build something of real permanence, with a spouse who was more devoted to her than some smorgasbord of addictions. A future where she could have a baby of her own.

"We don't have giant nurseries where the babies are turned out like some kind of manufactured good and then raised by nannies, Skye. Out here, babies arrive the old-fashioned way, and all that sacrifice creates a bond between mother and child that takes precedence over almost everything. There's a reason that Alexander has remapped your Society in such an unnatural way. He knew that real familial bonds were one of the few things that had a chance of breaking the web of addiction he was working so hard to create."

"So that was it? Katya fell in love with Jax and wanted a family and that was all it took for her to betray decades of indoctrination?"

Even as I said it I could taste the hypocrisy in my statement. I was shocked that Katya had forsaken the Society that had created her, but she'd had two reasons to my one. Why was I so astonished that Jax and a desire for a child of her own had been enough to turn her when nothing more than the chance of being together with Brennan had been enough to do the same to me?

"Not exactly, but it was the tipping point. Like I said, she'd already fallen in love with the culture Tyrell had created inside of his city, but she'd still planned on killing him. She would have too, except for the fact that she knew what it would do to Jax. Even back then, Jax was Tyrell's bodyguard and there was no way to get to Tyrell that didn't have some risk of Jax getting caught up as collateral damage."

"What did she do?"

Brennan reached over and took my free hand in his. "She went to Tyrell and told him everything. She didn't know who he really was, but she figured he was the one person who might be able to find a way to break her link back to the enclave.

"To hear Tyrell tell the story, he was more than just shocked when she came clean with him. He hadn't realized that Alexander had been sending human agents into the cities, but it explained a few things that had never quite made sense. More importantly though, for the first time in a century and a half, it provided

Tyrell with a chance to create an ally with a life expectancy as long as his."

"The serum. I understand now. Since she'd received the preparatory injections, there was nothing stopping Tyrell from upgrading her nanites to be just as effective as his."

It was nearly dark enough to make it impossible to see Brennan's expression, but I was pretty sure what I was seeing on his face was sadness.

"Nothing but a question of whether or not he could trust her. In the end, he did exactly that. He injected her with nanites from his own body that had been programmed to upgrade her computer and the manufacturing node that supported it."

"And she's been working with the two of you ever since."

"Not exactly. Katya ended up going her own way. I've never met her, but she's kept somewhat in contact with Tyrell. Things are still strained between the two of them as a result of her departure, but Tyrell still felt like we could count on her to get us out when Alexander finally decided to level this city."

Brennan's head was starting to bob, and I suddenly found myself wondering how long it'd been since he'd actually slept. Piter had probably kept him sleep-deprived while he'd been incarcerated, and it hadn't sounded like he'd had much of a chance to catch up on missed sleep between the time when he'd returned to the compound and our departure that morning.

I patted the ground next to me. "Go ahead and lie down, Brennan. Nanites are an incredible thing, but even they work best at repairing injuries while you're asleep."

"No, it's not fair to you. You've been up nearly as long and your injuries are even worse than mine. Besides, if I fall asleep up here I'll probably freeze to death."

"Not if I lie down next to you. It's still not going to be very comfortable, but my nanites won't let me actually freeze to death. I don't have the kind of control over them that Tyrell does, obviously, but they've been programmed to raise my core temperature in conditions much more extreme than what we should be facing tonight."

Brennan sat there motionless for several seconds before finally nodding and scooting away from the wall so he could lie down. I let him get settled and then lowered myself to the floor and rolled onto my side so I could maximize the amount of contact between our bodies.

I should've realized that he would be lying on his right side in order to keep his injury up away from the dirty floor, but somehow I'd been expecting him to turn so that he could see the door into our room. Rather than pressing the front of my body up against the back of his, I ended up face to face with him. It was simultaneously awkward and incredibly heady.

THE DESTROYER

The torrent of conflicting emotions raging through me meant that I wasn't as quick on the uptake as I should've been. If I'd reacted by turning over as soon as I realized what was going on I could've played it off as just me trying to get comfortable, but by the time I decided that I needed to roll over, it was too late to do so without making it obvious that I was trying to put some distance between us.

"I know what you're doing, Skye. This whole time you've been trying to distract me from the fact that I failed. Not only did I not manage to clear a path so that people could make it to the parking structure, I got the rest of our team killed and us cut off blocks from anyone who can help us."

I almost laughed in his face. He was giving me way too much credit. He thought I was concerned about his feelings, when the truth was that I hadn't stopped thinking about myself since the moment we holed up on the fourth floor.

"Actually, I really was just trying to get you to fall asleep. Even nanites can't keep you awake beyond what your body was meant to endure. I know our odds aren't good, but once it's dark the bad guys will have as hard a time seeing us as we'll have seeing them. We just need to buy ourselves some time to finish healing from the worst of our wounds, and then we can make a break for the compound."

"You're wrong. I've seen Tyrell stay awake for fifty-six hours at a time without any ill effects. I don't get the full benefit of his nanites, not without a computer of my own, but I don't have to sleep as much as a normal person. My borrowed nanites can still clean away most of the waste products that cause exhaustion."

There was something in his voice that I'd been having a hard time placing. He was obviously exhausted despite his protestations otherwise. That didn't make sense coming from Brennan, whose incredible intellect was only matched by his relentless honesty. Always before now, the truth had been his friend because only an understanding of the truth could allow him to perform his technological miracles, but something had changed. He wasn't just trying to convince me that he didn't need sleep, he was trying to convince himself.

I didn't respond for several seconds, and then suddenly it struck me. Brennan had experienced who-knew-what kind of terrors while Piter's prisoner, and now he was scared to go to sleep.

I couldn't blame him for his reluctance to close his eyes, but he needed sleep, and we were on a definite deadline when it came to getting back to the compound. If we didn't make it back before morning, we risked more than just being cut off from Tyrell and the others for another twelve hours. The Citizen-President would commence his attack around sunrise and we were going to need to be back at the compound if we wanted to make sure that we wouldn't be killed by a stray strike during the bombardment.

"Okay, Brennan. You don't need to go to sleep if you don't want to, but as long as you're awake I'd like to find out more about how you got here."

Brennan nodded sleepily. I couldn't see him even from just a couple of inches away, but I could feel his movements transmitted through his body and into mine.

"Tyrell found me designing booby-traps for a gang leader on the western edge of the next city he visited. I was only six, but I already had a good understanding of forces and how to construct simple machines. My parents were both out of the picture. I don't know if they died or abandoned me. All I remember is growing up around the fringes of the gang. There were a few good people who tried to make sure I didn't starve when I was younger, and then as I got older I was clever enough to find ways to make myself useful to the rank-and-file gang members."

"So Tyrell took you in?"

"No, not exactly. It was Jax who insisted I come back with them. They were out looking for usable machining tools. Even back then Tyrell had managed to establish a network of contacts throughout the world."

Brennan's answer surprised me. Somehow I'd never pictured Jax as a paternal kind of guy.

Apparently my surprise was easier to interpret than I'd realized.

Brennan patted me on the waist. "There's a lot more to Jax than meets the eye. Katya wouldn't have fallen in love with him if he hadn't shared her desire to someday have a family. They would've made a great couple if she'd stayed around."

"I guess that explains why Jax is so loyal to you—and why he's so bitter. Why didn't he go with Katya when she left?"

"She didn't give him a choice. One day she just up and left. She's talked to Tyrell since then, but she's steadfastly refused to talk to Jax."

Brennan didn't sound any less tired, but he almost sounded like he was starting to relax enough that he might be able to sleep. I wrapped my arms more tightly around him, pulling him close in the hopes that doing so would make him feel safe enough to finally drift off, but he misunderstood my intention.

Rather than tucking his head down against my arm, he looked up and suddenly our mouths were only millimeters away from touching.

My mouth was suddenly dry and my heart was racing. I couldn't remember ever being this nervous before, and even worse, our bodies were so close together that I was positive he could feel my heart trying to beat its way out of my chest. We remained there motionless for several long seconds before Brennan pulled back slightly.

THE DESTROYER

"Everything's gotten so confusing over the last couple of weeks, Skye. We knew that the ants were going to try to take my generator. I never actually expected to even get this far, but that was okay. Katya was going to come back and fly us up to the mobile command center in all of the confusion so that we could take it over and use it to shoot down all of the attacking aircraft.

"I knew going into this that Alexander was going to send an operative in. I was expecting a guy, or failing that some cold, emotionless bitch, but instead I got you, and you didn't just save my life, you seemed legitimately interested in trying to understand what we were accomplishing here.

"I wanted to tell you dozens of times that I knew you were the one who'd been sent to kill me and steal my generator, but the timing was never right. I'm so sorry for all the lies I let you believe. Do you think there's any chance of history repeating itself?"

My heart wasn't just pounding now, my body was shaking, and there was no mistaking the trembling as being caused by the cold. I was nearly positive I knew what he meant, but the thought of just coming right out and saying it was more terrifying than contemplating fighting our way back through blocks of hostile territory in the darkness.

"You don't have anything to be sorry for, Brennan. The lies you've told are nothing compared to the ones that I've told. I'm glad that you waited until the time was right to tell me the truth. If you'd broken your silence even just a day or two earlier than you did, I might have chosen to go through with my mission instead of risking everything to save you.

"I wouldn't change anything about what's happened over the last few weeks. I'm just glad all the secrets are behind us."

Brennan slowly shook his head. "I wish that were the case, Skye, but there's one more secret that Tyrell and I've been keeping from you. If he had his way it's a secret that you would never find out about, but I can't do that to you.

"Katya didn't just leave because she and Tyrell had a falling out, she left in pursuit of the very thing that had caused her to turn against her people. She wanted to have a family, but she didn't just want to be with Jax and her children for a few decades. Tyrell's injections had made her as immortal as he was, and she couldn't stand the idea of watching the people she cared the most about grow old and die.

"She left Tyrell and Jax so that she could sneak back into the enclave and have her baby there where it would have a chance of receiving the same preparatory serum that both she and Tyrell had been given. She and Tyrell don't see eye to eye on very much these days, but they continue to work together because they both want the same thing.

"Tyrell wants the secret of the serum so that he can give the gift of immortality to the entire world. Katya wants the serum so that she can give it to Jax."

I could see where Brennan was going with this explanation, and I suddenly felt stupid for not having seen it before then. The pieces were all there, and Brennan had been very clear with regards to Katya's driving force. It finally made sense. The strange bond I'd felt with the otherwise faceless parade of crèche nurses, the fact that I'd been told again and again throughout my life by a variety of people exactly what I'd needed to hear to be selected by the Citizen-President for this particular assignment, even the fact that I'd been saved by a random woman when someone in the military had tried to assault me.

It all pointed to the exact same thing. Katya had been successful in getting her daughter injected, but more importantly she'd been successful in keeping me away from all of the addictions so prevalent back in the Society.

Katya wasn't just some random woman who'd blazed the path of betrayal years before I'd been born, she was my mother.

Chapter 6

It went without saying that Brennan's confession ruined the mood. The news that I wasn't just a crèche baby like everyone else I'd grown up with rocked my entire world to the point where the last thing I was capable of thinking about was kissing Brennan.

I passed the first several minutes after Brennan's revelation in complete silence, unable to process everything well enough to manage anything remotely approaching speech. When I finally came back to myself, I realized that Brennan's breathing had deepened and slowed down.

Maybe he hadn't been scared of falling asleep, maybe he'd just been too weighed down by the last big secret he'd been keeping from me. For the briefest of moments I was tempted to be angry with Brennan for dropping that kind of bomb on me and then crashing like that, but the more I thought about it, the more I realized that I was looking at things the wrong way.

Brennan hadn't fallen asleep because he didn't care about me, he'd gone for far too many hours without sleeping precisely because he'd been too worried about me to let himself drift off until after he'd told me about Katya.

Instead of waking Brennan, I snuggled closer to him in an effort to keep both of us warm as the temperature continued to drop. The next two or so hours passed in a long, drawn-out blur.

There were simply too many important things competing for my attention. Was Jax my father? It sounded like Brennan and Tyrell had kept the true reason for Katya's departure secret from Jax, but that didn't necessarily mean that I should be doing the same. But was it really my place to be getting in the middle of everything? If Jax was really my father then it probably was, but there was no guarantee that anyone but Katya knew that.

That would have been enough to keep me unsettled for days, but there were also my feelings for Brennan to consider, the fact that I was getting sucked into the middle of a giant war, and the question of whether or not Brennan and I were even going to be able to sneak back to the compound.

The more time passed, the more I realized that last question was the one that I needed to focus on. I couldn't do anything about the rest of the things I was worrying about right now, but I could start trying to come up with a way to get Brennan back to the compound.

Given the fact that the Citizen-President would be landing troops onsite in the next seven or eight hours, getting Brennan to the compound wouldn't mean that he was actually safe, but I could only deal with one problem at a time. Once I got Brennan back to Jax and the others, I could start worrying about how we were going to survive what came next.

Lying there in the darkness next to Brennan's shivering form, with my arms wrapped around his bare upper body, was surreal in ways that I hadn't anticipated. Back in the enclave there had always been a clock nearby—either something mounted to a wall or the clock on my digital assistant. I'd spent a few terror-filled hours after I first arrived inside of the city without any way of telling time, but this was different.

When I'd been in Piter's territory, first fighting the fire and then trying to find a way across the makeshift wall that separated his area from Brennan's territory, there had been too much going on to ever worry about what time it was. I'd merely gone from one task to another.

Even once I'd made it into Brennan's territory and been forced to hole up while my body repaired my broken bones, time hadn't really mattered. I'd been free to let my nanites take as much or as little time as they required to get the job done.

THE DESTROYER

This was different. I couldn't go anywhere until Brennan had time to recover, but by the same measure we couldn't afford to remain where we were for too long. Once the assault started, our odds of getting killed by a stray attack would go up dramatically, but even if we managed to survive that, the Society's military would make sure that they controlled the high ground. It was going to be impossible to make it back to the compound if we had to dodge sniper fire the entire way.

To top it all off, I was starting to get tired. Under other circumstances that wouldn't have been a big deal. I would have set some kind of alarm to wake me up a few hours before dawn and we would have made our move then. Given that I didn't have any way of knowing how much time had really passed since sunset, I was operating purely on guesses when it came to deciding when we needed to get started back to the compound.

I knew it was going to be a futile exercise—there wasn't enough of the skyline visible through our window to use the stars as an improvised clock—but I opened my eyes and turned my head in an effort to catch a glimpse of the stars.

A flash of vertigo nearly made me vomit, and the discomfort finally pulled me away from my thoughts enough to register what was going on with my body. I didn't just want to throw up, somewhere in the last few minutes my shivering had ceased to be just about the cold.

I scoured my mind for possible explanations. Maybe a head injury could have caused it, but that didn't make sense. I didn't remember hitting my head hard enough for that, and even if I had, my nanites should have been able to repair that kind of one-time damage by now.

Some whisper of intuition made me reach down to the length of fabric I'd tied around my left leg. The material was wet, which was odd, but not entirely unexpected. Under normal circumstances, once I got any form of pressure on a wound, my nanites stopped the bleeding within just a minute or two, but the fabric I'd used had been awfully thin.

It wasn't until I brought my hand back up and caught a whiff of the stench coating it that I realized what was going on. I'd been poisoned.

I checked Brennan's side, but I knew what I was going to find even before I touched his too-cold skin. He'd been hit with the same poison, but unlike me, he didn't have a miniature factory buried inside of him that was capable of turning out a few million more nanites in short order to help fight off an unexpected invader.

A crushing torrent of despair threatened to shut down my mind, but I knew that I couldn't let myself give into the almost overpowering emotion. Brennan and I were both in incredible danger, and the only chance we had of surviving was if I kept my wits about me. I was going to have to think my way out of the hole we were currently in.

Based on what I'd learned since arriving in the city, Tyrell and Alexander had designed the nanites during a time when their primary concern had been fixing the things that the medicine of their time hadn't already been able to address. Cancer, autoimmune disease, stroke and heart disease, those were the kinds of things that they'd been targeting. The extra strength and speed that the nanites provided were a fringe benefit that they'd added in—probably on a lark.

Poisons were a relatively easy thing to cure once you knew what you'd been injected with. You just needed an antidote and a way to administer it—neither of which would have been a challenge for a society capable of engineering nanites and building the massive energy field that had protected Tyrell while he'd been doing his research.

Brennan's shivers had started out not much worse than mine were right then, but they'd already progressed to the point where they were nearly full-blown convulsions. That was both good and bad. I'd been injured before Brennan had, which meant his symptoms being more advanced than mine could only be due to the greater concentration of nanites in my blood.

That meant there was a good chance that Tyrell and Alexander had figured out a way to include some kind of resistance to this particular poison inside the bag of tricks that they'd programmed into the nanites. Unfortunately, whatever partial immunity I was enjoying didn't seem to have stuck to the same extent where Brennan was concerned.

There was no way for me to know for sure if that was because I had a much higher concentration of nanites in my blood, or if it was a side effect of me having been provided with a computer that was able to give the nanites more direction on an ongoing basis. If it was the former then Brennan was probably going to eventually pull through unless his nanites wore out or ran out of power before neutralizing enough of the poison that his body would be able to take care of what remained.

If, on the other hand, Brennan's nanites—superior though they were given that they were straight from Tyrell's own veins—couldn't deal with the toxin with whatever stock programming Tyrell had provided before drawing them out of his own body, then Brennan's only hope was for me to get him back to Tyrell before his system completely shut down.

Neither option was particularly good given the rapidly approaching deadline the Citizen-President had imposed on me. It was entirely possible that I was going to be just as much a wreck in six hours as Brennan was right then. If that was the case, then there was zero chance I was going to be capable of walking however many blocks there were between us and the compound.

Even if the poison ran its course much more quickly than that, I still didn't have any kind of guarantee that I was going to be able to get Brennan out of here in time. Even my nanites didn't provide me with enough strength that I was realistically going to be able to carry Brennan while fighting my way past an unknown number of enforcers.

That left only two options. I either needed to get Jax and the rest of the guards to come to me—a difficult proposition since I couldn't just pick up a radio and call them—or I needed to extend the deadline I was working against.

No matter how I tried to rotate the first solution, I couldn't make it work. Any kind of signal that I could possibly send to Jax would be just as visible to the enforcers I'd just spent so much time convincing Brennan and I were both dead. When you threw in the fact that anything burnable had been scavenged decades earlier, there just didn't seem to be any way to bring Jax to us.

That meant I was going to have to make another call to the Citizen-President. Luckily, I had the transmitter, but that didn't mean I was excited to be venturing back into the lion's den.

My shaking was a lot worse than it had been even just a few minutes earlier, which meant that I had a very limited window in which I would be able to talk to the Citizen-President and not sound like I was suffering from hypothermia. I reached into one of the cargo pockets on my pants and fished the transmitter out with fingers that were only a hair this side of completely numb.

I knew that neither Brennan nor I had made a concerted effort to move very far away from the wall we'd been leaning against, but it seemed almost too much to hope that I would be able to mount the transmitter to a piece of structural steel without moving. The relief I felt when one edge of the transmitter caught on a beam I couldn't see from where I was lying was almost indescribable.

Working off of nothing more than feel and memory of how the transmitter worked, I managed to get the other side of the transmitter secured on the opposite edge of the steel I-beam and then pressed the transmit button. Even as I did so, I realized that it was pointless to pretend I was by myself—Brennan was making far too much noise for that.

"Skinwalker calling Home Base, come in, Home Base."

The pause before a response came through was even shorter than I'd been expecting. Even more astonishing was that it was the Citizen-President who once again answered my transmission.

"This is Home Base. I was starting to wonder if something had happened to you, Skinwalker. Do you have a target for us as you promised?"

THE DESTROYER

"I'm sorry, Home Base, the situation down here has changed significantly. I think it can still work to our advantage though. The fighting inside of Brennan's territory has escalated remarkably quickly. As nearly as I can tell, warlords from every neighboring territory have decided to attack Brennan at the same time. Before I was sent out into the field, more than half of Brennan's guards had already been caught up in the fighting. Rather than attacking according to schedule, I think you should delay the operation for another twenty-four hours.

"As things stand right now, Brennan's people still have the ammunition and numbers required to make a strong showing outside of his compound, but that can't last for very much longer. It's going to be a little tricky timing everything correctly, but if I'm right, within the next day Brennan's forces are going to run out of ammunition and start taking significant losses. Rather than destroying the surrounding territories and then dropping troops in to the face of a relatively unbroken set of gunmen, we should hold off and let the enforcers from the other territories do the dirty work for us."

"There is some merit to your idea, but if we wait too long then we'll be faced with hundreds of knife-wielding lunatics with no home to go back to. I've seen the numbers and Brennan's guard contingent is much smaller on a per capita basis than anything you'll find in the other territories there. The last thing I want to do is trade in a fight I know I can win against a couple dozen tired, half-trained riflemen for a holy war against hundreds of hardened warriors."

I was having a much harder time following the conversation than I'd expected. Apparently the poison was affecting me even more significantly than I'd realized. I couldn't even remember if the Citizen-President had told me during our last conversation that he wanted Brennan alive or not. Despite the fuzziness in my head, I could tell that I needed a new line of attack.

"Yes, sir. If you feel that waiting is a bad idea, then I will do whatever is required to support the operation whenever you kick it off. Maybe it's for the best this way. With the inventor out of the picture right now, his men may not even make it another twenty-four hours."

It wasn't hard to let more of a tremble into my voice, instead the difficulty was in not letting it get too much too soon.

"Skinwalker, are you okay? Also, what did you mean about the inventor being out of the picture?"

Something told me that the Citizen-President resented the fact that he'd had to ask the questions in that order for the sake of appearances rather than being able to ask about Brennan first.

"The inventor went out to try to help push back some of the attackers and his squad was surrounded. His second-in-command sent me and a few others out with orders to sneak through enemy lines and recover the inventor, but my squad was cut to pieces. There's only me and one other guy left and we both got shot with arrows that had some kind of poison on them. He's not going to last the night, but I think I'll be okay in another few hours."

As I was talking, I was desperately trying to make sure I'd covered all my bases. Using the transmitter while there was anyone else around was a major breach of protocol, but hopefully something that could be overlooked given that my companion was supposedly only hours away from death. I was pretty sure I would be okay on that account, but nowhere near as certain that I'd played my cards in such a way as to convince the Citizen-President to delay the attack yet again.

The real question was whether or not I was correct to have believed Tyrell. If Tyrell was telling the truth, then the Citizen-President would do almost anything to get his hands on Brennan. The generator was still unfinished and there was no guarantee that anyone back in the enclave would be able to get it running without access to its designer.

Several seconds of quiet passed before the Citizen-President came back over the air.

"I've just cleared the room, Skinwalker. It is vitally important that you locate the inventor and stay by his side. When the attack launches I need you to get him to the dropship so that he can be secured at the same time that we secure the invention."

"I'll try, sir, but I don't know how long it will take for my nanites to get the best of this poison."

"You'll be up and moving around again just before dawn, unless it's one of the more exotic poisons in use down there. If that's the case you'll be up an hour or two before then. I can't delay the operation for an entire extra day—not with the way that everything is in motion down there—but I'll give you until sundown. I'm sorry, but that's the best I can do. I know that means you'll be forced to move through enemy lines in broad daylight, but we just can't risk waiting longer than that."

"I understand, sir. Skinwalker out."

The next few hours were a nightmare. My head felt like it was going to fall right off of my neck, and my joints ached. Actually, ached didn't even begin to describe it. They felt so swollen that I half expected my skin to burst from the pressure.

Somewhere along the way I'd lost my canteen, but Brennan still had his. As badly as I wanted to drain every ounce of fluid still inside of the metal container, I forced myself to only take a couple of sips. As terrible as I felt, I knew that Brennan had to be in a hundred times more pain. Nanites could do a lot, but the last thing I wanted was for his nanites to be exerting extra energy trying to compensate for the fact that he was dehydrated.

I fought through the alternating waves of fever and chill enough to sit Brennan up and slowly pour the contents of his canteen down his throat, praying the whole time that he wasn't so far gone that I was drowning him without even realizing it.

After that, I lowered Brennan back to the floor and wrapped myself back around him. The cold floor was sucking heat out of us, but all I could do was hope that my fever would offset his chills and vice versa.

My entire world shrank down to nothing more than the feel of his bare skin against my arms and the sound of his labored breathing. Every time his breath caught or his shivers got weaker, I worried that he'd passed the point of no return, but somehow he kept going, and the torturous hours until dawn slowly rolled past.

Going into the experience, I would've said that being forced to lie there next to Brennan, unable to do anything to help him, would have just made things even worse. It was bad, and the anguish every time he stopped breathing felt like actual torture, but somehow worrying about Brennan made the physical side of what I was going through easier to bear. I was so worried about him that my own pain became somehow insubstantial in comparison.

Apparently the enforcer who'd shot me hadn't used one of the more exotic poisons in circulation in the city, because I didn't start feeling well enough to even sit up, let alone walk around, until the eastern sky started to lighten outside the window. I checked Brennan for what felt like the thousandth time, and found that his condition seemed to have stabilized somewhat. He was still weak and shaking, but his breathing had evened out, and his wound had stopped weeping whatever noxious fluid was generated as a byproduct of the nanites breaking down the toxin.

I was worried about moving Brennan when he was still recovering, but I had a suspicion that the journey back to the compound was going to take an order of magnitude longer than it had on the way out here. Our only hope of getting back alive was if I moved from building to building whenever the coast was clear and avoided traveling on the streets any more than absolutely necessary. Given how much time we were likely to spend holed up in some building while we waited for groups of enforcers to move deeper into Brennan's territory, there was no guarantee that we would be able to make it back to the compound before sundown.

Even worse, there was no guarantee that Tyrell and Jax had even managed to hold the compound wall. If that was the case, I couldn't think of any way we could possibly get inside the compound. Unlike the ramshackle barricade that had separated Brennan's and Piter's territories, the wall protecting the compound was newly built and impassable without a lot more preparation and equipment than I had available to me.

I double-checked my knife, not that it would do me any good in a fight where the other guy saw me coming, and Brennan's rifle, which I couldn't use unless I wanted to have every enforcer within a three-block radius looking for us. Once both weapons were ready to go, I picked Brennan up and slung him across my shoulders.

He was lighter than I'd been expecting. I'd known my nanites would make it possible to pick him up and carry him however far I needed to go, but this was something else altogether. All I could figure was that the poison had taken even more out of him than I'd realized. His nanites must've been forced to cannibalize his muscle and bone mass in order to scavenge the materials they'd needed to keep him alive.

That only happened in extreme circumstances, and the fact that I didn't have any food or additional water to feed him made the situation even more worrisome than it otherwise would have been. If left unchecked, at some point his nanites would cause permanent damage in an attempt to keep him alive under circumstances where it probably would've been a mercy to let him die.

All of the deleterious long-term effects of prolonged nanite cannibalization ran through my head as I started down the stairs towards the ground floor, but I just kept telling myself that the only thing that mattered was that Brennan was still alive. If Brennan ended up paralyzed as a result of the poison, it wouldn't change who he was inside, and there was always a chance that Tyrell could program his nanites to repair the damage—assuming I could get Brennan back to the compound.

Once I made it down to the ground floor, I left Brennan inside the stairwell and crept out to the atrium just inside the main entryway. The metal plates that had been welded over the top of the holes that had once contained windows were a pretty good indication that this building had served as some kind of headquarters for one of Brennan's predecessors decades earlier, but they didn't do anything to make me feel safer. All they did now was block off my line of sight and make it so I had no real idea of what was waiting for me just outside the building.

I took a deep breath and then slowly nudged the front door open with my rifle at the ready. Even if I couldn't use it to shoot the bad guys, it would still be an effective club. Despite all of my fears, the street immediately outside the building was empty, and even when I leaned far enough out past the edge of the building to be able to see further down the road in each direction, there still wasn't any sign of the enforcers I'd been expecting to see crawling all over the place.

THE DESTROYER

I wanted to be optimistic about that particular development, but I just couldn't seem to get past the idea that it was a bad sign despite appearances to the otherwise. The most logical explanation for the lack of enemies in my immediate area was that the fighting had moved inside the compound during the night and there was no longer any reason for Brennan's rivals to maintain a presence out here.

I hurried back inside to collect Brennan and then made a mad dash to the building across the street from us. It wasn't ideal—I was headed east rather than north like I wanted to be—but unless I was ready to go strolling out onto one of the crossroads where I'd be exposed in every direction, it was my only option. All I could do was hope that one of the buildings to the east of me had a set of doors that opened to the north.

I had to travel through two more buildings before I found one that had a door on the north side. Every step of the way was nerve-racking, as though I was a lab rat who'd just been dropped into a giant maze—one with hardened killers potentially waiting for me around every corner.

I stopped leaving Brennan in one spot while I scouted the road ahead of me after the second building. I didn't like having to juggle his weight at the same time I slowly opened doors that creaked at the slightest movement, but I liked the thought of leaving him vulnerable on a floor somewhere while my back was turned even less.

I felt like eyes were watching me as I slowly went from building to building, but whenever I turned around expecting to find someone breathing down my neck, I was greeted with nothing more than empty space. The instincts that had gotten me into Piter's territory and back out more or less in one piece were screaming at me that I was being monitored, but I had no way of knowing whether or not that was just a side effect of the poison. My strength was back and I was able to walk in a straight line now, but my joints still hurt and there was a faint ringing in my ears that told me my nanites had not yet been able to completely eliminate all of the damage that had been done to me.

I'd been traveling for nearly an hour and a half, making my way slowly through the city, when it happened. I carried Brennan up to what was left of a door on the north side of a thirty-story skyscraper and started to stick my head through the giant hole that had once contained floor-to-ceiling glass doors when I heard a sound that didn't belong.

Acting without thinking, I retreated back inside the building and shifted to the side so that I wouldn't be visible from either of the two exterior doors in that area of the building. The way my heart was battering away at the inside of my chest made it hard to hear anything else, but I remained pressed against what was left of the marble facade on the wall I'd taken shelter behind. Nearly five minutes passed before I heard the sound again, and this time it was unmistakable. It was the sound of metal against brick.

There was somebody standing just outside the door, and I would've been willing to bet almost anything that they weren't on my side.

Possible responses flickered through my mind one after another as I tried to come up with a plan that gave Brennan and me a chance of making it past whoever was out there. If it was just one guy and I could take him by surprise, then there was every reason to believe I could kill him, but even then there was no guarantee that I'd be able to do it in such a way to prevent him from raising an alarm.

Judging by what I'd heard so far, it didn't sound like a large group, but all it would take was one extra person I wasn't anticipating for me to fail in my attempt at getting Brennan back to the compound. I considered trying to create some kind of distraction, but couldn't come up with anything that I could initiate from far enough away for the idea to have any chance of working.

That only left trying to go around, which I didn't particularly love. It had already taken longer than I'd been expecting to cover what little ground I'd managed since the sun came up, and it was only reasonable to expect that I was going to run into more enforcers the closer I got to the compound.

It was starting to look like the best I could hope would be to make it to within a few blocks of the compound and then try to use the distraction created by the Citizen-President's attack to make a run for the gate. The odds of that working were dismal, even if Brennan was recovered enough by then to make the run under his own power. Unfortunately, dismal odds were still better than sure death.

I shifted Brennan around on my shoulders, and then crept over to the door on the west side of the building. Knowing that I had enemies so close meant that I had to be even more cautious than I'd been up until that point. That meant moving more slowly and spending more time listening just inside doors before trying to scan the road visually.

I made it to the next building only to find that it didn't have a north-facing set of doors, and that I was going to have to move further west in the hopes of finding another route northward. I tried to tell myself that it would be okay. It had sounded like the enforcers I'd just left behind were standing close to the building I'd just vacated. That meant if I could get far enough to the west I might be able to cross the road heading north without them noticing me.

I worked through two more buildings before finding one with a door on the north side, and by then I was starting to feel desperate. Despite the risk in leaving Brennan unattended, I set him down in a corner of the entryway and slowly swung the door far enough open for me to slip out. I grabbed a chunk of nearby rubble and used it to prop open the door before moving closer to the street.

Based on the interior layout of the building, I'd known even before stepping outside that the doors on this particular building were set back more than twenty feet from the road. I tiptoed to the corner of the building right before it opened up to the street, and slowly stuck my head out to where I could scope out the road to either side of me.

Things were both better and worse than I'd been hoping. From my new vantage point I could see the source of the sound that had sent me more than three blocks out of my way. I'd been right not to try to continue north as I'd been doing. It hadn't been just one enforcer, there were three of them, and they looked like they'd been left behind as sentries. Two of them had located sizable pieces of asphalt and were using them as chairs within arm's reach of the building, but the third enforcer was standing further out into the road, slowly turning in place as though looking for something.

The only positive to the situation was that the road between the enforcers and me looked like it had been through a war. There were big holes in some sections and piles of rock and dirt in others, and it looked like if I timed my movements just right I might be able to get

Brennan across the road without any of the three enforcers noticing me.

I headed back inside, still moving quietly in case there were other enforcers nearby who I hadn't managed to pinpoint yet. I slipped through the door and then reached for my knife when I realized that Brennan hadn't been alone inside the building.

I had my knife clear of its sheath before it fully registered that the threat I was reacting to was a girl who couldn't have been more than six or seven, a girl who seemed to be trying to confirm that Brennan was okay. She turned to run, but I was faster, crossing the distance between us in two quick steps and gently grabbing her arm.

"I'm sorry, I didn't mean to scare you. You just startled me—I thought Brennan and I were all by ourselves."

She was shaking, obviously terrified, and I found myself in an unanticipated quandary. I had no desire to be traumatizing children, but just because she was a child didn't mean that she wasn't dangerous. If I let go of her arm there was nothing guaranteeing that she wouldn't turn and run away from me.

Even if she didn't mean any harm, all it would take was one misstep for her to lead enforcers back to us and get Brennan and me both killed. I sheathed my knife and gave her what I hoped was a reassuring smile.

"I want to let you go—I'm not going to hurt you—but I need you to promise me that you'll stay here and let me talk to you before you go running off. Can you do that for me?"

The nod I received was so tentative that it barely qualified as a sign of agreement, but we had to start somewhere. I held my breath as I let go of her arm and settled down onto my knees.

"Do you have a name?"

This time the nod was more emphatic.

"Will you tell it to me?"

I wasn't surprised when I didn't get a nod this time, but that didn't stop me from being disappointed. "Have you been following me for a while?"

Another nod, guarded as though she was worried I was going to be angry about that.

"Wow, I'm impressed. I kept thinking someone was watching me, but I could never find you. You must be really good at hide-and-seek."

This time I got a smile with her nod. I found myself surprised that I wasn't antsier about the delay she represented. There hadn't been very many children inside the compound—either because Brennan had felt like it was too dangerous of an environment for children, because Tyrell had been unwilling to feed and clothe people who couldn't help work, or simply because those with children had been unwilling to venture inside the compound.

Until I'd heard the story about Katya—about my mother—it hadn't struck me as odd that there weren't any children inside the compound. Things had been much the same back home on the other side of the barrier.

That wasn't to say that there weren't children inside the enclave, but the children were kept carefully segregated from the adults other than the few crèche nannies responsible for educating and caring for the rising generation. I was starting to get just the faintest glimmer of what Katya must have experienced when she'd first come into contact with the children during her mission to assassinate Tyrell.

"Shouldn't you be back with your family? Where are your mom and dad?"

Tears started trickling down her cheeks, as she shook her head, lips trembling. I felt like an insensitive oaf. The implication was clear; her parents had been killed in the fighting. I found myself wondering if they'd been killed while trying to work their way southward to the guard post where Brennan had planned on having everyone meet up.

The idea of being responsible—even indirectly—for making the girl an orphan wasn't a comfortable thought, but I forced myself to focus on the here and now. If I made a wrong move at any point during the next few hours the odds were very good that all three of us were going to die.

"I'm trying to get somewhere safe. Would you like to come along? You'd have to be very quiet and do exactly as I tell you or else the bad men will get us."

It was hard to tell whether she was nodding or shaking her head. I got the impression she wasn't sure what her answer was either. I tried again.

"Would you like to go somewhere safe?"

A yes, and an emphatic one at that.

"But you don't feel like you can come with me? Even if I say it's okay?"

A no, but this one seemed to indicate there was room to negotiate the response. I could hear Brennan shaking behind me, but it sounded like he was still breathing, so I continued to focus on the little girl. I'd never appreciated how difficult it was to communicate with someone who was limiting themselves to yes and no answers.

I'd just about given up and then it suddenly came to me.

"You're not by yourself, are you?"

She shook her head again, and this time she looked scared. As worried as she'd been that I was going to hurt her, that was nothing compared to her concern for whomever she was trying to protect.

"It's okay. I trust you not to run off and tell the bad man that my friend and I are here. You can go get them. Are they here in this building?"

She looked deep into my eyes and I got the feeling that she was trying to read my soul. Up until that moment, I hadn't even been truly convinced that I had such a thing as a soul. I probably couldn't have agreed to the Citizen-President's mission if I'd believed in that kind of thing at the time, but as she looked at me from a distance of only two feet, I found myself hoping that I hadn't done anything that would irreparably stain whatever she was trying to see. I couldn't save her or her friend if she didn't trust me, but I wasn't sure that anyone could trust me if they knew how many people I'd killed in just the last few days.

I tried to put on a reassuring smile, but even as I did it I knew my expression came out more sad and regretful than reassuring. Somehow it passed muster though, because she smiled in return and then turned and hurried over to a half wall on the other side of the room.

A couple of seconds later she led another girl out into view who looked like she could've been the first girl's twin. I wanted to cry, but I knew that wouldn't help the situation. Those two dirty, half-starved girls needed me to be strong. If I broke down and lost it there deep in the middle of hostile territory, it was almost certain that they would fall apart as well.

I had to be strong for them and Brennan both, but I didn't know how I was going to get all four of us back to safety. I wasn't going to leave them though, so I had no choice but to try.

"Okay, the four of us are going to go out through that door to the north. There are bad guys off to the east who we don't want to see us, so we're going to hide behind the rocks in the street. I'm going to go first with Brennan, and then once I'm across to the other side, the two of you can come along behind me. Watch how I move and be careful to only move when I give you the signal, okay? It's kind of like a moving game of hide-and-seek, do you think you can do that?"

I got an enthusiastic nod from the first girl, and a weaker—but still determined—nod from the second girl. There wasn't anything else I could do to prepare them—at least not in the time I had left. It was time to make a break for it.

I readjusted my rifle, hanging on its sling, and then picked Brennan up. He felt a lot lighter than he should've been, but worrying about him wasn't going to get us back to the compound any more quickly.

I brought my finger to my lips, reminding the girls to be quiet, and then led them out to the door on the north side of the building. It only made sense that the two of them were capable of moving quietly—they'd followed me without making enough noise to alert me to their presence—but I was still taken by surprise at how lightly they stepped.

I'd never been anywhere near that quiet when I'd been their age. Apparently that was one of the differences between growing up in a war zone and growing up inside of a controlled environment where you are protected from everything likely to hurt you.

I edged just far enough around the corner to confirm that the three enforcers hadn't moved and that the one on guard duty was looking the other direction, and then started across the street, staying as low as possible in an effort to make sure I wouldn't be seen if he turned.

The trip was a lot harder than I was expecting it to be. The human body had never been meant to run hunched over like that, and I was also torn between keeping both eyes on the enforcer and watching the road ahead of me well enough to avoid tripping over something and falling to the ground in the kind of crash that would garner exactly the kind of attention I was trying to steer clear of.

I ended up settling for mostly watching the ground, but stopping before each of the big gaps between one set of cover and the next to make sure that the enforcer didn't show any signs of being about to turn in my direction. It was a compromise between speed and safety, but it managed to get me all of the way to the other side of the road and into the shelter of the other building without being noticed.

I lowered Brennan to the ground just in front of the doors, and then moved back to where I would be able to see the enforcer. I'd been moving slow and keeping my head down where it was less likely for him to notice me, but I still felt my heart nearly leap out of my chest when it turned out he was looking in my direction.

I stopped moving, figuring that it was better to hold still even if I was technically out where he could see me than it was to move and risk his eyes being drawn directly to me. The next twenty seconds as he scanned the terrain in my direction seemed to take forever to pass, but he finally turned back in the other direction, and I realized I'd been holding my breath.

I waited a few heartbeats to make sure that he wasn't about to spin back around to catch us moving now that we felt safe, and then waved the girls forward. They were short enough that they didn't have to bend down to remain hidden behind the rubble in the road, but that didn't stop them from doing exactly that. The pair of them ran while holding each other's hands, bent forward at the waist in an attempt to mimic exactly what I'd been doing.

I'd been subconsciously counting under my breath ever since the enforcer had looked away, and I suddenly realized I was nearly back up to twenty seconds again. Acting on a hunch, I held up my hand for the two girls to stop behind one of the bigger piles of rock on the road.

There was no guarantee that he was sticking with the twenty-second span of time before checking out the other half of his surroundings. In fact, a good guard probably would've made a concerted effort to avoid settling into any kind of predictable routine, but I was betting that that was exactly what he'd done.

The girls skidded to a stop, eyes darting desperately from side to side in an effort to identify any possible threats, and then a split second later the guard turned in our direction. I resumed my slow count, doing my best not to let my anxiety influence the rate at which I was counting, and right on schedule the enforcer turned back in the other direction.

I started to wave the girls forward again, looking over to find that the first girl had edged just far enough around the cover they were hiding behind to be able to see the enforcer. The second girl started forward in an effort to comply with my instructions, but her friend pulled on her hand, yanking her back behind cover before she could take more than half a step towards me.

I looked to my left just in time to see the enforcer whip his head back around in our direction. This time he watched for nearly a full minute before turning away from us, and it was clear to me that he'd caught some kind of movement during one of his previous scans. He was a lot better of a sentry than I'd given him credit for, and if it hadn't been for the first little girl going against my orders so she could watch him as well, he would've caught us.

I watched the enforcer for nearly five seconds before turning back to the girls and giving the first one an inquiring look. Apparently whatever had tipped her off to the fact that the enforcer had been about to turn wasn't being repeated, because she nodded and pulled her friend into motion.

The fact that we'd waited longer than normal to get the two of them moving again, combined with their shorter legs, meant that they couldn't make it all the way to me in one quick burst, but that was okay. They stopped three-quarters of the way across the road behind a piece of asphalt that would never have had a prayer of hiding both Brennan and me, and then continued across the road, reaching me safely the next time the enforcer turned his back to us.

"That was gutsy, little girl. I'm impressed—I should've realized just how much spunk you had to have had in order to make it this far all by yourselves."

My comment earned me the biggest smile I'd seen out of her yet. I couldn't help but smile in return.

"If you're still unwilling to tell me your name, do you mind if I call you Spunk?"

She smiled and pointed to herself as though pleased with the moniker. I turned to the other little girl, at a loss for what to call her, and then shrugged.

"And until one of you tells me otherwise, you'll be Tiny."

Tiny didn't acknowledge my declaration, but I wasn't entirely surprised. Whatever they'd been through had obviously been hard on her, and she didn't seem to be handling it as well as Spunk was. If there was something I really needed to communicate to her I was pretty sure I could manage it, but for the most part it seemed like as long as Spunk understood what was going on, she was more than capable of keeping Tiny out of trouble.

We started through the building in front of us, moving as carefully as we could considering I was still carrying Brennan and apparently had never had a good enough reason to learn how to move as silently as Spunk and Tiny. Thankfully, this was another building with doors on the north. Knowing that we might not have to backtrack for at least a couple more blocks was an incredible relief, but I didn't let that lure me into overconfidence.

Once we made it to the door, I stopped and listened for nearly a minute in an attempt to determine if there was another batch of enforcers waiting just outside the building. I didn't hear anything, and Spunk gave me a thumbs up when I gave her a questioning look, so I once again lowered Brennan to the floor and then motioned for the two girls to stay and keep an eye on him.

After visually confirming that the coast was clear, I went back for Brennan and the girls and we hurried across the street, arriving safely inside our target building. We moved along in much the same manner for nearly an hour and only managed to make it across two more blocks, and both of them involved heading east rather than north like we needed to be going.

I hadn't realized just how spoiled I'd been early on in the trip. We'd gone from massive buildings that took up the entire block and which had easy access from one set of doors to all of the rest of the egress points, to smaller buildings, many of which only had one set of doors that faced the street.

That meant we were spending a lot more time crossing alleys full of improvised housing or moving along the street to get to the next set of doors. It was nerve-racking, and not just for me. I could see that both of the girls were uneasy with the idea of spending so much time outside and exposed.

We'd been forced to double back so many times that I was starting to lose track of where we were in relation to the compound. I knew it was generally northwest of us, but I wasn't sure if we'd already gone far enough north to run into it if we went further west, or if going west would just result in us crossing the breadth of Brennan's territory without actually running into the compound.

Somewhere along the way I'd lost count of how many blocks I'd moved east versus how many blocks I'd moved west. I wanted to keep moving north, but so far there hadn't been a good chance to do so, and we were starting to see more signs of recent fighting.

Just in the last block alone we'd had to detour around two different groups of dead enforcers and one corpse that had been wearing a guard uniform. If I'd been by myself I wouldn't have bothered detouring, but I didn't want to expose the girls to any more death than they'd already seen. I was going to have to make a difficult decision soon though.

I led the girls inside of a bigger building and then set Brennan down for a moment so I could stretch and catch my breath.

"If we keep on like we are, I'm afraid that we'll miss the compound. I know it's dangerous to go through the crossroads, but we're going to have to head north soon. Do you think the two of you can keep going?"

Tiny's slow, hesitant nod nearly broke my heart, but even Spunk's response was showing enough exhaustion that I could tell she was reaching the end of her strength. I couldn't blame them. I was dehydrated enough that my nanites were probably swimming around in red sludge, and it was very possible that the two of them had gone longer without food and water than I had. Unfortunately I didn't have anything to give them, and that wouldn't change unless we made it to the compound.

I waited another couple minutes, hoping it would be enough for the girls to recuperate some of their energy, and then picked Brennan back up and headed outside. Our street was still clear for as far as I could see, but the closer we got to the crossroads the more nervous I became.

We were only twenty feet from the end of the block—already able to see sizable chunks of the crossroad we were approaching—when I heard movement ahead of us. It was the worst possible place to be caught by enforcers. There was no way we could make it all the way across the street to take cover in the building over there, and there was very little cover on our side of the street.

I looked backwards, confirming what I already knew. The last doorway we passed was more than fifty feet back; there was no way we were going to make it back there in time either.

Our only hope was a doorway into what looked like the remnants of a sandwich shop, and it wasn't very promising given that it had sported massive windows all along both exterior walls.

I whispered for the girls to run and took off at the fastest pace I could manage without alerting whoever was coming around the corner as to my presence. It only took me a couple of seconds to make it to the door, and I thanked my lucky stars that the door had been glass as well. Not even one in a thousand windows had survived two decades after the Desolation, and this door was no different. That meant it was a simple matter for me to squat down and step through the door without having to open it and risk an ear-shattering squeal as the ancient, corroded metal protested being moved again after all these years.

I shoved Brennan underneath the table in the closest booth and turned to help the girls. Spunk managed to make it to the door without any problems, but for the first time she was more focused on our danger than on keeping Tiny out of trouble. As soon as she was through the door her pace picked up and that caused her to pull Tiny off balance just as the younger child was trying to go through the door.

Tiny started to fall and tried to catch herself, but the only thing within arm's reach was a jagged shard of metal that cut her hand open. She cried out, and I knew we were in trouble.

Her yell hadn't been particularly loud—it had come out sounding as frail as she looked—but there wasn't anything between us and the enforcer I could hear moving towards the sandwich shop from the crossroad.

Based on how close his footsteps sounded, I had only a split second in which to react. I scrambled across the filthy, dangerous floor and took cover underneath the opposite row of booths, heedless of the way I'd just sliced my hands open. The girls started to follow me, but I motioned them to get under the booth next to Brennan.

Nearly all of my attention was focused on what was coming next. I had my knife out ready for use, but even just the split-second glance I'd spared to make sure that Spunk and Tiny had made it under the table was enough to cut big slices out of my heart. Spunk was back to looking terrified and Tiny was vainly gripping her hand in an effort to staunch the bleeding that had already painted a big chunk of her clothing red.

I could see in their eyes that they thought I was about to sacrifice them to save myself, but there wasn't time to explain. I couldn't afford to have them staring at me, so I pointed up at the window above me with a scowl that I hoped would scare them into looking where I wanted them to look.

Spunk went white and instantly looked away from me, but Tiny just started sobbing. Any chance of our escaping notice went out the window once Tiny started crying, but I couldn't bring myself to be mad at her. Her entire world had been shattered over the last few days, and now she was injured and scared while the one person she'd been counting on to get her to safety treated her like this had all been her fault.

"Do you guys hear that?"

"What, more rats?"

"It's not a rat. That sounded like something else. Something bigger."

The first speaker sounded frustrated like this wasn't the first time his companion had shrugged off his concerns.

"I don't know, man. They've got some pretty big rats over here. If there was any doubt about just how rich this Brennan guy is, it was settled for me the first time we ran into a rat that looked like it could carry off a small baby. Our rats back home never got that big. What do you think he's been feeding them?"

"Probably idiots like us who are too stupid to realize just how outmatched we really are."

The first guy's response had been said practically under his breath as he reached the door closest to me, so I knew the other guy hadn't heard it. He pushed the door open with an unpleasant squeal of metal on metal, and then stepped inside.

From my position underneath the table I couldn't see much of what was going on, but I could practically feel his thoughts as Tiny's cries lured him further inside the shop. He only took one step before realizing how unlikely it was for two girls to be hiding there all by themselves. His weapon, a big ax that had seen better days, came up as he finally saw Brennan, but by then it was too late.

I lunged forward and sank my knife into his thigh, targeting the large artery just below his pelvis.

It was a poor choice given how long it would take him to bleed out even from such a large blood vessel, but it was the best option I had open to me given just how poor my starting position was. He yelled, which I fully expected, and started to bring his ax down towards my head as my knife struck.

What I didn't expect was the way that my blade sheared entirely through the back of his leg. I'd done a lot more than just sever the artery I'd been aiming for, I'd destroyed his ability to support his weight with that leg, and he started falling.

I brought my right leg forward and kicked off against his right leg, knocking him to the ground at the same time that I threw myself out of the path of his ax. He hit a pile of scrap metal with a loud clatter, and then I was on my feet, bending down to pick his ax up off of the floor.

I'd managed to kill him without taking any injuries, but he'd raised the alarm, and I heard his partner bellowing as he came running in my direction. I had a sneaking suspicion that I'd just kicked over a hornets' nest.

The second enforcer had nearly arrived, and I realized that my original plan of trying to lead him away was too dangerous. I just couldn't risk the possibility that they wouldn't stay focused on me. I was going to have to beat a hardened killer on his own terms with a weapon that I didn't have any experience with.

I spun back around just in time to see the second enforcer come through the door, and I brought my ax up as I jumped backwards to dodge the first swipe of his club. It was tempting to haul back and swing my ax at the newcomer with all of the force I could muster, but that felt like the wrong answer. I was faster than he was, but if I committed myself to the wrong attack that wouldn't do anything to save me.

His club was shorter than my weapon, which meant that he didn't have my reach, but it also meant that he would be a lot faster than a normal human wielding something as big and heavy as my stolen ax. He lashed out at me a couple of times driving me backwards, and I let him. I continued to back away, trying to develop a feel for how fast he was and what kind of attacks he favored. I let him continue to advance until my back foot brushed up against a pile of garbage that I remembered seeing just in front of the door.

I was out of space and time with which to take my opponent's measure. I made as though planning on stepping backwards again and then reversed direction at the last second and slammed the blunt head of my ax into my opponent's throat. My attack was too tentative to crush his throat like it should have, but his club dropped out of position as he started choking and my kick took him in the knee with devastating results.

My instructors back home would've taken his head off as he dropped. There was a lot to be said for making sure that he wouldn't be coming back and giving us problems in the next few hours, but I couldn't bring myself to do it.

THE DESTROYER

Maybe it was because I knew the two girls were watching. They both had doubtlessly seen more than their share of death and blood since the invasion had begun, but the last thing I wanted to do was scar them even more than they'd already been scarred.

Maybe that wasn't even the cause. It was entirely possible that I was getting tired of killing people as well. But for whatever reason, instead of hitting him with one of the sharp blades on either side of the ax head, I slammed the butt of the ax into his temple with enough force to make sure he would be unconscious for at least the next couple hours.

"Get to your feet, both of you. We've got to get out of here before anyone else shows up."

I dropped the ax and picked Brennan back up, slinging his familiar weight across my shoulders as I headed towards the door we'd just entered from. I was worried about the cut on Tiny's hand. As weak as she was, it was entirely possible she would bleed out in the next little while if I didn't get her wound bandaged up, but if I didn't get us somewhere safe in the next few minutes we were all going to die.

I threw the door open and stepped out onto the street to find that we had enforcers approaching both from the north and the south.

"Hurry, around the building and go to the left."

Spunk and Tiny took off at a run, but they were no match for my longer stride. I arrived at the corner a couple of steps ahead of them to see that the compound was visible off to the west for the first time since I'd set out that morning, and that there was a massive group of enforcers between us and the compound. I looked back to the east, but it was only marginally better. There were two enforcers approaching from that direction, and both of them looked like they were armed with slings. Our only hope was to cut through the enforcers between us and the compound.

There was no point trying to keep a low profile anymore, so I brought my rifle up tight against my shoulder and started picking off enforcers out of the group between us and the compound. I dropped my pace down to something only slightly faster than what the girls could manage so as to give myself a better likelihood of hitting what I was aiming at.

"Stay with me, girls."

I half expected them to refuse to follow me into what I knew was nearly certain death, but I'd been hoping that the fact I was in the lead would keep them moving. The selector on my rifle was set to single shot, and in between strokes of the trigger I was able to hear two sets of tiny feet pounding along on the pavement behind me.

Some combination of my training back in the enclave had combined with Jax's instruction and my experience during the prior forty-eight hours to make me a better shot than I had any right to expect. I'd prioritized my targets starting with anybody carrying a distance weapon, and all of my first three shots took their targets in the center of their chests.

Two riflemen and an archer were down for the count as we hit the halfway point of our current block. I fired off two more shots, aiming at the two guys who looked like they were most likely in charge of the group, and felt a piece of hot brass strike my cheek as it was ejected from my rifle.

I could feel Brennan starting to slip, but tried to get another shot off before slowing down to shrug him back into position. It was a mistake and that shot completely missed its target. At that point every bullet was priceless, but I refused to let the miss shake my concentration.

I was out of obvious targets, so I started prioritizing based off of who was in the lead. It wasn't going to make much of a difference with regards to when I was going to be within striking range of one of those wicked-looking swords, but I figured there was a chance that watching the people in front of them hit the ground in a spray of blood might cause the enforcers at the back to break and run.

It wasn't a very good chance, but it was all I had left. I certainly couldn't fight someone hand-to-hand while carrying Brennan and leaving him behind would just make everything I'd tried to do since I'd arrived in the city pointless.

Something hit the ground only a couple of feet from where I'd been about to step, and as shards of rock cut into my legs I realized that the sling-wielding enforcers behind us had made it into range. If it had just been me I probably would've taken my chances. Hitting a running target at almost any range was difficult, and there was a decent chance that I could survive anything but a direct hit to my head or chest. Unfortunately, the girls weren't nearly as fast as I would've been by myself, and they wouldn't recover from the kind of hits that I would have been able to shrug off.

I turned and put a bullet into each of the sling users, but I knew I was just delaying the inevitable. Those two enforcers had had the range required to take shots at us, but the rest of our pursuers were gaining on us quickly. It was going to be a matter of seconds rather than minutes.

I spun back around as the girls passed me and started to slow down.

"Don't stop running! Even if something happens to me you have to get to that wall. Get to the wall and then turn and run along it until you find a gate. Tell whoever you see there that Brennan and Skye sent you."

I saw movement out of the corner of my eye up on the compound wall, but I had no way of knowing if the force gathering up there was made up of friends or foes. I fired off three more shots in quick succession and dropped three more enforcers, but I knew I'd started out with less than a full magazine and there were still more than a dozen men between us and safety—even assuming we were going to be capable of outrunning the ones behind us.

The smell of hot lead and gunpowder was sickly sweet at the back of my throat as I squeezed the trigger four more times and dropped three more enforcers—two of them fatally—and then the bolt on my rifle locked back. There was no longer any reason to hold my speed down, so I lengthened my stride in the hopes I would be able to get enough of a lead on the girls to punch a hole through the approaching horde of enforcers.

I dropped Brennan in the street five feet before I ran into the first opponent, and a tiny part of me died as I did so. I was sentencing him to death. I could hear the enforcers behind me approaching quickly and there was no question but that they would make sure of him as they ran past, but I couldn't fight while carrying him and a hard, pragmatic part of me knew that neither he nor I was going to make it out of this alive. The best I could hope for at that point was that the enforcers would focus on me so that Tiny and Spunk would be able to make it past them.

There was so much adrenaline in my system that my heart sounded like a drum beating only inches away from my ears, but even if that hadn't been the case, the sheer volume of rifle fire I'd just exposed my ears to would've still left me the next best thing to temporarily deaf.

Something felt more than heard tore past me at such incredible speed that there was a noticeable shockwave in the air next to my head a split second before I got into range of my first opponent. He was short compared to what I'd come to expect from an enforcer, but he wielded a spear with a speed that had to be seen to be believed—only I was even faster than I expected to be.

I spun to the side as he stabbed at me, and knocked the point of the spearhead away from me with my rifle before continuing my spin inwards and slamming the butt of my rifle into the side of his neck. I heard his neck crack with the finality of someone who wouldn't ever walk again, and then plucked his spear out of the air before it could hit the ground.

It was foolish to let my rifle drop back down to the end of my sling and replace it with a weapon that I'd never used before, but something about the decision just felt right. Despite my incredible speed, I couldn't survive in a close-quarters brawl against multiple opponents who were all bigger than me and armed with edged weapons. I needed the extra reach that the spear offered.

The roar in my ears had only gotten louder, but I didn't need my sense of hearing to fight this particular battle. When the people pursuing the girls and me caught up with us I was a dead woman—I just needed to make sure that I opened up the hole the girls needed before that happened.

I thrust my spear forward, taking a tall guy with a mace through the chest, and then used the shaft of my spear to knock another enforcer's sword thrust out of the way. There wasn't time to get the point of the spear back into play, so I slammed my foot into the sword-wielder's leg and then slammed the shaft of my weapon into his face as he started to fall.

The enforcers were spreading out in a half circle—trying to pin me against the building to my left so that more of them could attack me at the same time—but they'd made a mistake. There weren't as many of them as there should have been, which had to mean that some of them had gotten overeager and gotten too far ahead of their fellows. I could work with that.

A flicker of movement brought me around just in time to dodge an ax blow that would've split me in half down the center. I spun underneath the end of my spear and then ripped it free of the first enforcer's chest so I could slam the blunt end into the ax wielder's chest.

They were in too close now. I used the shaft of my spear to block another attack—this time from someone wielding a two-handed sword that sheared more than three-quarters of the way through my weapon. I kicked another enforcer in the stomach before he could get the ends of his daggers into me, and then spun my spear around like a bo staff.

The thick wooden shaft less than a foot behind the head of the spear slammed into the head of the swordsman who'd just taken a swing at me with enough force to simultaneously knock him unconscious and snap the wood where it'd been cut midway between me and the point of impact. I was now left with nothing more than my bare hands and a pointy length of wood only slightly more than four feet in length.

Another enforcer, this one with a metal club as big around as my leg, took a swing at me, but I shot forward and slammed the sharp end of my stick into his chest a split second before he would've connected with his blow. Now that I was inside the arc of his attack, it was a small matter to shrug off the impact as his forearm slammed into my shoulder.

Unfortunately, by then the guy with the knives was back. I'd kicked him, but I'd been too rushed to give the attack as much force as I would've liked. He feinted with his blades and then lunged forward intending on opening me up from crotch to shoulder. I spun around to the outside with all of the nanite-infused speed I was capable of, and still almost wasn't fast enough to survive his attack.

I felt a tug on my stomach as the point of his blade sliced a furrow half an inch deep through my tender flesh, but by then I had hold of his wrist and it was a simple matter to slam my open left hand into his elbow and shatter the joint. The knife wielder gamely tried to spin back around so that he could get his other knife into play, but his damaged limb simply gave me too much control over the rest of his body.

I jerked him off balance, pulling him towards me a split second before I slammed my fist into the side of his neck. He went down in a boneless heap and then I was forced to throw myself to the side in an effort to avoid a slash from yet another guy with a sword.

This guy was the biggest specimen I had gone up against yet, but I got the feeling that he was used to substituting strength for technique. His slashes were powerful, blindingly fast attacks, but he was putting too much into them. Maybe if he'd been trying to cut through armor it would've been prudent to use so much force, but all it was going to do against someone like me was leave him open on the back half of his swing.

I jumped backwards, hoping that I wasn't about to trip over Spunk or Tiny, and then reversed direction as soon as his sword was even with me. I couldn't have moved any sooner than I did, but even so I was almost too slow. He'd already reversed the direction of his swing by the time I got to within arm's reach of him, and I wasn't positive—even with my nanites—that I was going to be strong enough to block his arm as he brought his sword back around, but I didn't have any other choice.

I slammed my open palm into his wrist hard enough that I felt some of the bones in my hand and wrist fracture, but even that was nothing more than an attempt to buy myself some time. The swordsman screamed in pain and I caught a flicker of movement as his sword started to drop away from his now-useless hand, but I'd already bent my knees dropping my weight down and forward as my right fist slammed into his crotch.

A tiny part of me knew that I'd neutralized this opponent, that he was no longer a threat with a broken wrist and crushed genitalia, but my training took over as I straightened my knees, launching myself upwards with a single explosive movement. My left foot pushed off of his knee as my undamaged right hand reached up and cupped the back of his head a split second before I slammed my right knee into his face.

I landed on both feet with my left hand down at my side and my right raised to ward off a series of attacks that never came. I surveyed the ground around me in a semicircle expecting to find another half a dozen enforcers queuing up to fight me and instead found only corpses.

The thunder in my ears had mysteriously all but disappeared sometime between when I'd grabbed that spear and when the last body had hit the ground, but there was still an occasional crack coming from off in the direction of the compound. A flash of movement off to my left caused me to look up at the compound wall just in time to see a fresh round of flashes that could only signal ongoing gunfire.

All of a sudden the object that had gone streaking past me made sense. By that point I'd killed both of the slingshot users behind me as well as both archers from in front of me, but I'd assumed one of the other enforcers trying to catch up to me must've had a bow as well. Only now that I thought about it, the projectile I'd seen had been moving in the wrong direction. It hadn't come from behind me, it'd come from in front of me—from the compound wall.

For one terrifying split second as I turned to run back for Brennan and the girls, I was convinced that Tyrell and Jax had lost control of the compound wall and that the gunmen up there shooting at me were a bunch of enforcers. About the time I reached Brennan and the girls passed me, I realized that didn't fit with everything else going on. Whoever was up there hadn't shot me yet, but they had gunned down half a dozen enforcers who'd come within a hair's breadth of overwhelming me.

I looked back to the east and rather than seeing another dozen enforcers rapidly closing in on me from that direction, I saw nothing but empty road interspersed with more corpses. I picked Brennan up, grimacing in pain as my broken wrist was forced to help support his weight until I could get him draped across my shoulders, and then followed the girls toward the compound wall.

We weren't out of the woods quite yet—the guards on the wall wouldn't still be firing if there weren't enforcers trying to get at me—but it was very much looking like we were going to make it back to the compound alive.

Chapter 7

Tyrell was waiting for me when I made it to the compound gate. Tiny had lost so much blood that she was starting to fall behind Spunk, but now that I had covering fire from above I was able to pick her up with my right hand and carry her the last hundred yards. I half expected for one of us to take an arrow before we made it inside the compound, but the rifle fire somehow managed to keep what was left of the enforcers busy long enough for us to make it to safety.

"What's happened to him?"

I handed Tiny to one of the guardsmen with Tyrell and then lowered Brennan down to the stretcher they'd brought. "Poison. He took an arrow to the side, but I got that out and got the bleeding under control. I think he's on the mend—or at least would be if I hadn't dragged him through a war zone—but there wasn't anything else I could do for him out there in the field."

Tyrell checked Brennan's pulse and then apparently decided that he wasn't in immediate risk of dying. "Okay, let's get him down to my room. I've got something that should get him back on his feet before the sun goes down."

A nearby guard handed me a strip of cloth as one of Tyrell's men set Tiny down so that he could grab his end of the stretcher. I picked her back up as I pressed the improvised bandage against her cut.

"Come on, Spunk."

"They aren't coming with us, Skye."

"Yes, they are. You don't have to let them into the secure area of the headquarters building, but surely there's someone back there who can watch them. I didn't bring them all this way just to have you throw them back outside the wall."

Tyrell had the grace to look embarrassed. "Nobody's talking about sending them back out into that. You can bring them along, but I'm holding you to your promise not to bring them into the lower levels."

I wasn't sure what I was expecting to see when we got to the headquarters building, but it definitely wasn't the sight that was waiting for me. Someone had taken massive bolts of fabric and strung them from the headquarters building out for dozens of yards in several different directions so that they were ten or twelve feet off of the ground.

It wasn't until I saw the people moving back and forth from the headquarters building to the bore that I realized what was going on. Tyrell was trying to defeat the Citizen-President's satellites.

As we got even closer I was able to see that the stream of people and equipment was coming directly out of the secure entrance.

"Why exactly are you worried about two little girls going down there when it looks like you've already got half of the compound traipsing around inside your precious secure area?"

Tyrell shrugged. "It's not half of the compound. It's a specially selected group that are as close to being perfectly vetted as I've been able to manage so far, but I take your point."

I was nearly ready to ask him if that meant I could keep Spunk and Tiny with me when Lexis saw us and hurried over.

"Oh my goodness! Is Brennan going to be okay? And where did you find these two poor things?"

I nodded. "I think Brennan will be fine, he seems like he's already through the worst of the poison. As for your other question, this is Spunk and this is Tiny. I caught them following Brennan and me back to the compound this morning. So far they haven't said a word, but when I asked Spunk about going back to their parents she shook her head like it wasn't possible."

Tyrell pointed to the girls. "Lexis, would you be so good as to make sure that they are taken care of? I'm going to need Skye's help administering an antidote to Brennan."

"Of course, I'll take care of them myself."

Spunk looked like she was nearly ready to start throwing punches, and Tiny grabbed a hold of me with the kind of desperate, fragile strength I suspected could only be managed by a child. I bent down so I could meet their eyes.

"This is Lexis. She's my friend and you can trust her. I would go with you, but I need to make sure that the bad men can't get past the walls. Go with Lexis and be good girls. She won't let anything happen to you, and I'll come find you as soon as I can."

Neither girl looked particularly happy to be separated from me, but they let Lexis pick them up. She promised to have someone bandage Tiny's hand, and then walked away with the two tiny figures before I could say anything else.

Tyrell hadn't stopped to wait for me, but it still only took me a couple of moments to catch up with him and the others. Even then, most of the delay came from dodging people headed the other direction. Some of the equipment they were carrying looked awfully familiar, but I held my tongue until we were inside Tyrell's room and he'd dismissed the two stretcher bearers.

"You're moving all of Brennan's equipment into the bore, aren't you?"

"Yes. It was never supposed to come to this. We were supposed to have more time before Alexander escalated things to this level, but with Katya having gone dark our only hope of preserving any of this is to seal it in the bore."

As Tyrell spoke he pulled out a syringe and stuck it into one of his veins. I watched as he withdrew several cubic centimeters of blood and then injected it into Brennan. Tyrell took three more blood draws before he was satisfied that he'd bolstered the number of nanites inside of Brennan's system sufficiently.

"They'll have to do. I just hope it's enough to get him back on his feet before Alexander sends his troops down. By the way, do you know what's going on there? You originally said that the invasion was supposed to happen this morning."

I nodded. "Yeah, that's my fault. Our team got pinned down and the other three got killed before we could make it to the southern guard post. Brennan and I retreated into the building where I picked off a bunch of enforcers and staged things to make it look like we'd been killed.

"My original plan was to wait until just before dawn for the two of us to try to sneak back to the compound, but once I realized that we'd both been poisoned, I called back to the Citizen-President and convinced him to extend the deadline."

"And how exactly did you do that?"

I was starting to get tired of all the questions, but I knew I had to keep Tyrell happy if I wanted to be able to stay with Brennan. "I told him that my original plan of luring all of the guardsmen into a single location so he could take them out with a single orbital strike wasn't going to work, but that I had a better idea. I told him that we were in a fight for our lives down here, and that every hour he delayed would mean more of Brennan's guardsmen would be dead and he would be up against less resistance when he finally landed troops."

"That doesn't seem like the Alexander I remember. He liked sure things as much as anyone, but he was always smart enough to know when to pull the trigger on something rather than waiting so long that the opportunity passed him by."

"As I was saying, I told him that we were fighting off all of the enforcers within a forty-block radius, and that Brennan had been captured again. I didn't come right out and say it, but based on what you told me earlier, I knew that Alexander wasn't going to land his troops and risk losing Brennan if there was any other way. He wants the generator and he knows that nobody inside of the enclave is going to be able to get it working for him."

Tyrell gave me an appreciative look. "That was very well done. How much time did you buy us?"

"I tried for another twenty-four hours, but I'm afraid all I managed was a twelve-hour extension. Is that going to be enough time for Brennan to be up and moving around now that you've given him a fresh batch of nanites?"

Tyrell shook his head. "I'm not sure. Without knowing what the two of you were exposed to, there's no way to know how much damage the new nanites are going to have to repair. Even if I knew what was used on him, I still wouldn't know how many nanites he had in his system when he was injured."

"So give him more of your blood. If four injections isn't enough to get the job done, then go ahead and give him four more."

"It doesn't work that way, Skye. If he had the full nanite package—a manufacturing node combined with a neural computer—then more nanites would speed the process because there would be something there to give his nanites intelligent direction. Since he doesn't have that, there's no mechanism to address multiple issues at one time. The injections I've already given him are more than enough to deal with the most pressing issues, and a trillion more nanites would just circulate uselessly through his blood waiting until his body stabilizes enough for them to be able to identify the next system that needs work."

Tyrell checked Brennan's pulse once again and then turned as though planning on leaving. I grabbed his arm before he could take a second step.

"Hold on, where are you going?"

"I'm headed back upstairs so that I can have someone signal for Jax to come back to the compound."

"You mean he's not here right now?"

My feelings were too mixed up to know for sure how much of my concern related to the fact that we were going to need Jax once the ants landed troops, and how much of it had to do with the possibility that he was my father. Either way, I wasn't happy to hear that he was out there somewhere, potentially pinned down by the same kind of overwhelming force that had nearly killed Brennan and me.

"Of course not. Brennan can issue whatever orders he wants to, but that doesn't mean that Jax is going to obey them. It was all I could do to keep Jax from taking half of our men and leaving the compound as the sun went down last night. When he got back here and found out that I'd allowed Brennan to go out into that madhouse with only four guards, I half expected Jax to shoot me.

"I managed to convince him to wait until morning, but there was never any doubt but that Jax was going to go out looking for the two of you. The southern side of the compound has been under near-constant attack since shortly after the five of you left yesterday. It's no wonder you were cut off and pinned down. Jax took a force of twenty-five guardsmen and headed out to the east intending on curving down around to the south once he was past the biggest concentration of enemies."

"You can get him back though, right?"

"We arranged a set of signals before he left. I'll go have someone shoot off the appropriate number of flares to let him know that you and Brennan have returned safely to the compound."

Tyrell looked at my hand on his arm as though expecting me to let go of him, but I couldn't bring myself to let him end the conversation that quickly. I knew he could easily remove my hand from his arm if that was what he wanted to do, but at that moment physically holding on to him was my only way of getting my questions answered.

"What happens next, Tyrell?"

He opened his mouth as though to dismiss my question, and then stopped and rubbed his temples. "To be quite frank with you, Skye, I don't know. It will at least partly depend on how many people Jax has lost out there today, but given our current force levels, I don't think we have any real chance of fighting off the ants when they start landing. Our tentative plan of trying to take over one of their troop transports is looking less likely to succeed with every guard we lose out on that wall."

"If fighting isn't an option, what does that leave?"

My voice came out as something only barely more than a whisper, but Tyrell didn't seem to have any problem hearing me.

"If fighting isn't a possibility, then the only course left to us is to try to hide. We'll scatter our people around the periphery of the compound and hope that Alexander isn't feeling particularly bloodthirsty today. With any luck he'll come down, disassemble Brennan's generator and then take it back up to his mobile command center, leaving whoever survives the bombardment to try to rebuild some kind of life down here."

I shook my head. "That's never going to work, and you know it. He wants the generator, but the generator does him no good without Brennan. It's not going to be possible to flee across what's left of the city—not with their snipers and drones circling over the wreckage—which means that the ants have nothing but time. They'll torture everyone else down here if that's what it takes to find Brennan—dead or alive."

"So we won't tell anyone where he is. The people in Brennan's territory can't give up what they don't know, even under torture. We'll hide him and wage a long-term guerrilla war on the ants."

Tyrell was shaking, but for once it didn't seem like his anger was directed at me. He was just as frustrated by the situation as I was, but unlike me he was refusing to face the facts. For a single heartbeat I was tempted to accuse him of refusing to fight because that was the course most likely to allow him to survive what was headed our way.

If we put up too much resistance then the ants would be tempted to just lift off and bomb the entire compound back to the Stone Age, but if we went to ground and Tyrell changed his face there was every reason to believe he could hide until Alexander found Brennan and left having gotten everything he wanted.

The temptation to make the accusation was almost overpowering, but I didn't. I stopped myself because I was finally realizing why Brennan had been able to get away with dictating terms so often to Tyrell. Tyrell didn't just view Brennan as a gifted protégé, he viewed him as the son he'd never had.

"Is that what Brennan would want? Do you really think that Brennan would be okay condemning hundreds of his people to that fate?"

"No, we both know he wouldn't, but with any luck by the time he regains consciousness, it will be too late. The decision will already be made and he'll be stuck with it."

I laughed, but it was a bitter, almost mocking sound. "Yeah, because Brennan is exactly the kind of guy to let something like that stand. You know better than that, Tyrell. Once Brennan realizes what you've done—what we've done—he'll march himself straight to the ants' dropship and hand himself over.

"He'll justify his actions based on the fact that he doesn't matter in the grand scheme of things. He'll tell us that as long as you make it out of there alive he can die happy. As long as that happens, you'll be able to continue working against Alexander and hopefully someday defeat him. Brennan was willing to risk his life to get the people outside of the compound into that parking garage. His feelings for those people are nothing compared to how much he cares for you, Jax, Lexis and the rest of the people he's spent so many months working with."

Tyrell tore his arm free of my grasp, but he didn't make any move to leave the room. "Listening to you is like hearing my own words repeated back to me, Skye. Everything that you've said is true, but I refuse to accept a future in which Brennan sacrifices himself to save the rest of us. I will keep him in a drugged stupor for months if that's what it takes to save him."

"He'll never forgive you."

"That is a price I'm willing to pay. There's no other way to keep him alive."

I ran one finger down the side of Brennan's face and then took a deep breath. "There's another way, but you're not going to like it. I'm not sure that even the prospect of saving Brennan will be enough to make you agree to what I'm about to propose."

"Try me. When you've been alive for as many years as I have, you realize that there is very little you won't do under the right circumstances."

"You're already planning on sealing the bore; do you have enough explosives to bring this building down as well?"

For the first time in our acquaintance, I'd managed to truly surprise Tyrell. I could see the wheels turning inside his head as he tried to come up with a reason to destroy the building we were standing under.

"Yes, if there were actually a reason to do so, but all that would do is destroy the generator and make Alexander even more desperate to get his hands on Brennan. I fail to see how that would help us."

"It will help us because it means we'll know exactly where the bad guys are going to be. The Citizen-President didn't say that they were bringing multiple dropships down, he said dropship—singular. We can work with that. I'm going to need every spare weapon we have. Don't disarm any of the trained guardsmen, but other than that, the rifles are all going to come with me."

"You're right, I don't like this. I don't even need to hear the rest of your plan to know that I'm not going to approve of it."

Tyrell turned to go, but I once again grabbed his arm. He spun as though planning on punching me, but I blocked the blow and threw an arm bar on him, forcing him to the ground.

"You can refuse to help me—I can't stop that—but you will listen to me. If you'll give me all the spare rifles and as many guard uniforms as we can find, then I can make it look like Brennan is with me when I lead all of the noncombatants to the southern end of the compound. Based off of everything you've told me so far, the Citizen-President would never let himself be put in a position where he wasn't surrounded by guards and sure of his safety. He'll never believe that someone like Brennan would send the bulk of his guardsmen away like that. He'll be positive that Brennan is with me.

"Meanwhile, you, Brennan, Jax, and the real guardsmen will hole up somewhere close enough to this building that the bolts of material you've got hanging in the air will hide the fact that you went there. You'll wait until they bring the dropship down and disembark the bulk of their troops, and then you can launch a surprise attack to take over the dropship and use it to get away from here."

I had Tyrell's face pressed into the concrete beneath us, but that didn't stop him from being able to talk. "What's the catch, Skye? You said that I wouldn't like your plan, but so far there's nothing to dislike."

"The catch is you have to make it so that I have a chance of saving those people. I won't knowingly lead Lexis, Tiny and Spunk to their deaths. We'll go find the tunnels that Piter used to kidnap Brennan, and work our way out to the outer edge of Brennan's territory. With any luck once you're gone the ants left on the ground will have their hands full fighting whatever enforcers survive the bombardment, but even if that's true I'm going to need an edge if I'm to have any hope of killing whoever ends up coming out on top down here."

"You want me to upgrade your nanites. What's to stop me from refusing to do that, but using the rest of your plan anyway? With the rest of our people serving as a distraction, there's a very real chance we could take over the dropship Alexander's people come down in. Turning you into an even better killer doesn't have to enter into the equation."

I applied a little more pressure to Tyrell's arm and smiled at the hiss of pain that I drew out of him. Tyrell might be right in his belief that Alexander needed to be killed, but that didn't necessarily mean that I liked Brennan's mentor as an individual.

"You're going to upgrade me because that's the only chance you have of Brennan not hating you when this is all over."

"You really think that you're that important to him? Frankly you're—"

I cut him off before he could finish whatever insult he had planned. "Actually, I do think that I'm that important to Brennan, but even if I wasn't, it still wouldn't make any difference.

Unlike you, Brennan cares about the people out there. Guardsmen, textile worker, farmer, it doesn't matter, they're all important to him. You're going to upgrade my nanites because that's the only way to give those people a chance of surviving, and whether or not they have a chance absolutely matters to Brennan."

I'd said my piece, so I let go of Tyrell's arm and moved back far enough to give myself a chance of getting out of the way if he tried to hit me again. I half expected him to leap to his feet and do his best to kill me, but instead he pulled himself to his knees and then stayed there on the floor looking up at me.

"Brennan really was right about you. You've completely switched sides. Alexander no longer has his hooks in you, does he?"

"What was your first clue? The third time I saved Brennan's life, or the fact that I didn't kill you just now?"

"Neither. Alexander is more than capable of ordering someone to do all of those things if he thought it would give him what he wanted."

I was starting to get exasperated. "What then?"

"It was the fact that you chose to go with Brennan yesterday even after you found out that I was the Destroyer. Even after finding out that I have the secret of immortality swimming around inside my bloodstream, you were still more concerned about Brennan than you were about keeping tabs on me. That's not the action of someone who's still working for Alexander."

"I did just demand that you inject me the same way you did Katya. Isn't it possible that I went off with Brennan, called the Citizen-President, and got a set of instructions to that effect?"

"No, the last thing Alexander would've wanted was for there to be another person running around with the same abilities as him. He would've known that I would only give you the kind of upgrade that I gave Katya. That will make you faster and stronger even than him, but it won't give you the ability to do the same thing to other people. Alexander would've wanted you to either kill me the first chance you got, or not let me out of your sight so that he could capture me and try to break the encryption on my neural computer. You're the real deal, and if you're still willing to give us a chance to take over the dropship, I will happily inject you with a set of nanites designed to take your performance to the next level."

Chapter 8

It wasn't until after Tyrell had injected me with thirty cubic centimeters of blood that I remembered how long it'd taken my initial injections to create the manufacturing facility and neural computer that allowed me to function at a higher level than the individuals who received the standard military nanite pack.

"How long do you think it's going to take for your nanites to do the job? This plan kind of falls apart unless I become a lot faster and stronger within the next few hours."

Tyrell patted me on the shoulder as he put his syringe down and then covered Brennan with a blanket. I still didn't feel like we were particularly close, but apparently now that he was convinced of my devotion to Brennan, Tyrell was willing to let bygones be bygones.

"The bulk of the changes should only take another half hour. It will probably take you some time to access all of the capabilities your new computer will provide you, but the hardware will essentially be all squared away with plenty of time to spare before our deadline."

"What about production of the new nanites? It can't be that easy. I remember it taking days before I noticed any kind of real change the first time around, and to hear Brennan talk about it, your nanites—just as much as the neural computer and the capabilities it adds—are in a whole different class."

Tyrell nodded. "That's true, but you're not starting from zero. Brennan never doubted you, Skye. I didn't share his confidence, so I refused to give you the full upgrade, but he did convince me to make some preliminary changes while you were unconscious after rescuing him. For the last twenty-four hours, a few million of my nanites have been hard at work upgrading the infrastructure inside of you. You may have noticed that you were a little faster, or that some of your senses were more acute, but that will be nothing compared to what you're going to be capable of by the time the sun starts going down.

"Now, if I don't get out there and have somebody signal for Jax to return, this crazy plan of yours will never even get off the ground." Tyrell turned and walked away from me, but then paused at the door out to the hall. "Before this is all said and done, you may very well curse me for what I just did, but I hope you don't. Immortality is an awful burden, Skye. If you survive the next few hours, I hope you bear your burden well."

I spent the next two hours at Brennan's side desperately hoping he would wake up before it was time for me to go, but even my worry for him couldn't completely distract me from what was going on inside of me.

This wasn't the first time that I'd been injected with nanites designed to make fundamental changes to my body. I'd half expected for this to be no different than what had happened to me back inside the enclave, but that turned out not to be the case.

I was right in thinking that I would feel stronger and more energetic, but I wasn't anticipating the way it would feel as the connection between my nerves and the neural computer began changing. It had taken me days the first time around to train my neural computer to trigger the one facial reconstruction that had come along with the version of nanites that the Citizen-President had injected into me.

This time things were much different on that front especially. As I focused on a particular section of my body it seemed like I had an extra sense tucked away in the back of my mind. If I focused on my legs I was presented with a...menu...of options that my new hardware was capable of implementing in that area.

THE DESTROYER

Some of them were blindingly obvious, if completely impossible to describe in terms anyone else would've been able to understand. The first option, one that came across something like a lemony taste that left prickles of heat on my tongue, was like having an instant shot of strength to the muscles in that location.

There was a cold, salty sensation associated with another of the selections, but when I tried to choose that particular augmentation I got a strong sense that the computer didn't think that I needed to use it right then. My best guess was that I'd just tried to activate some kind of healing protocol, but there was no way to be sure without slicing myself open to see.

As tempting as that was, I didn't feel like I could afford to waste any of the nanites currently swimming through my body. Tyrell had seemed fully confident that he'd injected me with more than enough nanites to see through the changes to my internal hardware, but with my luck even the smallest amount of blood loss would result in me losing critical amounts of his nanites and never having the upgrade process complete.

I knew that was ridiculous, but even ignoring that consideration, I was only hours away from a pitched battle with men running nanite protocols only a few generations behind my own. It would be a tragedy if I died because I came up a few hundred thousand nanites short when it came time to seal off some life-threatening wound.

Around monitoring Brennan's condition to make sure that he was continuing to improve, I started experimenting with the rest of the options presented to me by this newer version of my neural computer. I found out that my new nanites were capable of speeding up my mental processes by at least a factor of two. That combined with the improved reaction time once my nanites plugged into the long neurons running from my brainstem out to my limbs meant that I was now in a completely new league when it came to how fast I could absorb and then react to outside stimulus.

Improved vision—vision so good I suspected I would be capable of seeing a bullet travel through the air—was another improvement that I'd acquired as a result of my spinal set of injections, as was the ability to change my face nearly at will. When I discovered the location of that last menu, I tore myself away from Brennan for nearly half an hour while I experimented trying on different looks. All that was required to completely change the underlying bone structure and look of my face was to visualize how I wanted to end up looking. Somehow the nanites and the neural computer translated that into the trillions of instructions necessary to realize my new vision for myself.

By the time Tyrell finally sent someone down to check on me, I was torn between the desire to stay by Brennan's side and needing to get out where I could experiment with my new capabilities. I was guiltily relieved to be able to order Tyrell's messenger to stay and keep an eye on Brennan so I could go up and talk to Tyrell.

Tyrell gave me a knowing look when I tracked him down inside of the large tent he was using as a command center. "I'm sure you've got a lot of questions. Hold on while I clear everyone out of here."

I waited until the two of us were alone before starting with the first question on my list. "Is Jax back yet?"

"Yes, and I've fully briefed him on our plan. It's going to be touch and go with the number of men we've got left, but I've already injected him and two of his most trusted lieutenants with doses of nanites programmed to increase their reaction speed. The fact that his two subordinates don't know what they were just injected with won't have any effect on how well the nanites work. If we can get a couple of lucky breaks and take the ants by surprise, I think we'll be able to take the dropship."

"Good. How many extra rifles were you able to round up?"

"We raided the armory for both working rifles and units that were being used for spare parts. All told, you'll have twenty working rifles at your disposal and another thirty that will look like they function from a distance. We've had our munitions factory going full speed since shortly after Brennan was kidnapped. We've still gone through ammunition faster than we've been able to turn out new rounds, but we've got enough left to send you out with two hundred rounds per functioning rifle.

"I would send you with even more, but we both know it's unlikely to make a difference. Besides, if things go poorly with the attack on the dropship, we could go through several thousand rounds in very short order."

I nodded. "Okay, I can work with that. What can you tell me about my new capabilities?"

"Probably less than you would like to know. As much as I would like to claim otherwise, creating the connection between your neurons and your computer is a very complicated procedure that I was not able to reduce to a perfect science before the Desolation.

"So far Alexander, Katya, and I all share a broad selection of benefits as a result of our upgraded nanites. Prolonged life, increased strength and reaction speed, and the ability to change our appearance are all roughly the same across each of the recipients so far. The computer, on the other hand, starts with similar baseline programming and identical capabilities, but it will tailor itself to your individual circumstances."

I shook my head in confusion. "I don't understand what that means."

"I'm afraid I can't tell you any more than that. I designed the neural computer's software to be self-modifying, but without more data than I have access to there's no way to be sure what that will mean in the long run."

"Okay, what else? Is there a limit to how many protocols I can have running at the same time? If so, why?"

"Yes, there is. My early work showed that there is a limit to how many nanites the human body is able to support at one time. Obviously your body would cease to function if there was so much metal in your bloodstream that your heart was no longer able to circulate your blood, but it's even more than that. My latest generation of nanites goes to great lengths to collect energy from the circulation of blood to your body, but that isn't sufficient to keep everything up and running like it needs to be—at least not without changing the structure of the nanites to the point where they would individually be much less effective than they are now."

"So where's the rest of the energy coming from?"

"Directly from your central nervous system, which means that there's a different kind of limit on how much energy can be drawn out and dedicated to powering the nanites swimming around in your blood."

"So since there can only be so many nanites inside my body, there's only so much they can do at any one time."

"Yes, that's correct. As you get more experienced at interfacing with your neural computer, you'll find that you're able to split your nanites between different tasks, which will allow you to do more than you can do right now, but there's still a limit to how many different protocols you can have operational at any given time."

"But I could inject my blood into somebody else to give them temporary benefits, right?"

"Yes, if you survive that long, then you'll be able to inject nanites that have been programmed for specific functions into those you trust. It's simply a matter of choosing a protocol but instructing the computer not to activate it."

"And how do I do that?"

"You have to learn how your computer interfaces with you over time, Skye. I wish that there was a manual I could give you, but each link is simply too unique for something like that to work. Trust your computer—its ability to learn is remarkable, and even I can't predict just how powerful your particular link will become. I never expected that I would someday be able to access the manufacturing node inside of me with sufficient control to experiment on the structure of the nanites themselves. Given enough time you may accomplish something even more amazing."

Before I could ask anything else, a familiar voice called out for permission to enter. Tyrell looked at me questioningly, and I nodded. I still had questions that I wanted answered, but it was becoming apparent that Tyrell couldn't give me the kind of information I was after. Besides, the person entering the tent was someone I'd been hoping to see before I left.

Jax looked back and forth between Tyrell and me before clearing his throat. "I owe you my thanks, Skye, for getting Brennan out of there alive yet again. He's more than just my boss, he's—"

"The son you never had. I understand. I'm glad that you were able to make it back here to the compound. Did you lose very many out there?"

"Not as many as we lost here on the walls last night, but more than I would've liked. Tyrell briefed me about your conversation with Alexander. It's actually a good thing that he's not going to delay the attack as long as you asked him to. I don't think we could last another night against what's out there."

I nodded, unsure what to say. Brennan and Tyrell had let Katya—my mother—keep him in the dark for more than seventeen years. Did I dare tell him that I might be his daughter? I wanted to, but doing that would have consequences.

Unlike Tyrell, I wasn't prepared to condemn hundreds or even thousands of innocents to death in an attempt to save Brennan, but that didn't mean that I wouldn't do everything else in my power to try to keep Brennan alive. Jax was a big part of keeping Brennan safe, and there was a chance that my telling Jax the truth about Katya and the fact that I was her daughter would ruin that.

Tyrell had already injected Jax with a dose of nanites in an attempt to make him the equal of the ant military personnel he would be fighting in just a couple hours. If I told Jax that I might be his daughter, he might very well refuse to stay with Brennan. As much as I would welcome Jax's presence at my back during the fight I was headed into, Jax couldn't be with me and with Brennan at the same time.

I tried to tell myself that Tyrell could always just inject somebody else, but he'd obviously reached the limit of how many nanites he could afford to pull out of his own body and still maintain the edge he needed in order to survive what was coming. It was the only explanation for why he hadn't augmented more than just Jax's two lieutenants.

It was a good thing that I'd already made my decision regarding my role in the upcoming fight before I saw Jax again. If I couldn't tell him the truth right now, the next best thing would've been to simply send Lexis and the others off to their deaths while I stayed with Tyrell, Jax and Brennan, but I knew that would be wrong.

In the final analysis, it turned out that I was a lot more like Katya than I realized. We were both more maternal than anyone would've expected out of a couple of ants—the difference was I wasn't willing to abandon the children already here in an effort to grant just one child the possibility of immortality.

All of that went through my mind in a split second as my nanites reacted to my subconscious desire to speed up my thought processes. I looked at Jax and realized that there wasn't anything else to be said. Instead I reached forward and shook his hand.

"Good hunting out there. I'm counting on you to keep Brennan safe, he's better than all of us."

"I will. Thank you for what you're doing. About an hour ago we managed to find the entrance to the tunnel that Piter used to kidnap Brennan. I've detached one of my men to make sure that you find it without any problems. I wish I could do more."

"You've already done everything that could be expected under the circumstances. I suppose I'd better go see to Lexis and the rest."

I nodded at Tyrell and then turned and left the tent. It was time to go find my people.

Chapter 9

It turned out that somebody had already passed all of the necessary orders to the rest of the compound's residents. I exited the tent to find a group of more than four hundred people waiting for me.

Lexis was at the front with Spunk and Tiny hiding in her skirt. Behind her was arrayed a group of fifty guardsmen in ill-fitting uniforms who looked like they'd never held a weapon before. I took it all in along with the boxes of ammunition and the packs full of food and water that nearly everyone was carrying, and then cleared my throat.

"I'm sure you all have a lot of questions, and what answers you've received so far probably don't make a lot of sense. The truth is that I'm not sure I can do any better explaining what's going on than the people you've already talked to. All I can say is that in the next hour the ants are going to be coming for all of us. At this point nobody has a particularly good chance of surviving to see tomorrow, but our best hope is for us to take shelter in a tunnel we've recently discovered at the south end of the compound."

I expected protests or at the very least questions from the group before me. They all had eyes and could see that our guards had no more training than Lexis, but all I got back in response to my comments was quiet acceptance.

Lexis seemed to understand my confusion. "Tyrell told us that this is your plan, but that Brennan supports it fully, and says that it really is our best chance. That's good enough for all of us."

There was a low rumble of agreement from the rest of the group, and then Lexis shouldered her backpack and set off towards the south end of the compound without looking back to see if anyone else would follow. I accepted a new rifle and all the ammunition I could carry from the guardsman that Jax had detached to get us to the tunnel, and then headed off to the south.

The trip to the decaying building containing the tunnel went by faster than I'd been expecting. All too soon I found myself following our guide into a tangled warren of jagged metal and broken glass. The deeper I got into the building the more shocked I was that Jax's people had managed to find the entrance to the tunnel that Piter had used to abduct Brennan.

Our guide seemed to sense my amazement and pointed to a complex series of painted symbols on the floor. He held up an old-fashioned propane lantern—one of several dozen we'd been provided with—and pointed at the floor. "We must've spent the better part of a thousand man-hours in here mapping this place, but once you understand our methodology, things get a lot easier."

He was right, it took only five minutes for him to explain how to read the guides they had left at each crossroad, and after that I was reasonably confident I could make my way around inside of the building as long as I had enough light to see the symbols. That was a big relief—I didn't want to have to fight a rearguard action inside of the tunnel where most of our people were going to be, but I equally couldn't fight a battle inside of the building if I couldn't navigate without getting lost.

I'd had only the barest beginnings of a plan when I'd set out from the command tent, but by the time we arrived at the stairs down into the basement of the building I had a pretty good idea of the best way to proceed. I knew time was short, but I headed downstairs and then followed our guide through another collection of metal and garbage that was just as impenetrable as the one we'd left behind on the ground floor. I needed to make sure that I was back topside in time to position those few qualified riflemen I'd been provided, but it was equally important to get a sense of the terrain I might end up retreating through if things went as badly as I expected them to.

Apparently there had been a different group responsible for mapping out the basement—that or they'd just been paranoid enough that they'd thought it a good idea not to use the same set of symbols on both floors. The route from the stairs to the gaping hole leading down to the tunnels was more direct than the one we'd had to navigate upstairs, so just a short time later I climbed down into the tunnels.

I'd been expecting another parking garage, similar to the one the insurgents inside of Piter's territory had used as a training facility, but this looked more like the remnants of a subway tunnel that had been abandoned long before even the Desolation had taken place.

I turned to our guide. "Did you guys map it all the way to the other end?"

"No, there simply wasn't time before the compound came under attack. We know it has to come up somewhere though or they wouldn't have been able to use it to get Brennan out of the compound."

I nodded as I inspected the men standing before me in guard uniforms. There wasn't a lot upon which to judge their skill levels, so I just picked two of the younger, more nervous-looking of the company.

"Okay, this is what we're going to do. I want the two of you to take your weapons and begin working your way down that tunnel. With any luck the group that took Brennan through here left some kind of discernible trail. If that's not the case then you'll need to start mapping out our surroundings, but whatever you do, don't get too far away from this point until after the bombardment is over."

"How will we know when it's done?"

"This will be unlike the bombings you're used to. It won't be firebombs—it'll shake the very ground for miles in every direction and lay waste to most of the city. We shouldn't have to worry about direct damage for several blocks in any direction, but I would hate for you to be taken out by a stray strike."

"Understood. We'll go just far enough to make sure that all of our people can make it down into the tunnel."

"Good, but as soon as the ground stops shaking you need to get everybody moving. I have a sneaking suspicion that the ants won't be too far behind their bombardment, which means we won't have as much of a lead as we would like."

I turned to the second group of men who were likewise dressed in guard uniforms, but whose rifles were obviously nonfunctional. "I want all of you to maintain order down here and keep people moving so that there's room for the new arrivals."

"What about the rest of us?"

THE DESTROYER

I gave them my most confident smile and pointed back upstairs. "You're my wolves. Let's get back upstairs so I can show you what you're going to do."

I was surprised at how orderly the procession down into the tunnels was. We passed Lexis, Spunk, and Tiny on our way back up out of the hole, and I wanted to stop and wish the three of them luck, but I knew I couldn't. Too many lives depended on me getting the rest of these men deployed where they would have at least a slight chance of taking out some of the ants.

Once we were back on the ground floor I pointed at the stairs. "My plan hinges on maintaining control of the safe way back and forth from here to the floor above us. I'm sure you noticed on the way in just how many holes there were in the ceiling above us. What you may not have realized is that we're going to be fighting enemies with the capability to see in the dark, a capability we don't share—yet."

I pointed at a handful of the older men. "I want you all to take two lanterns apiece and go put them out in strategic points on the first floor. Try to position them so that they're sheltered behind something that will stop a bullet, and then get some flat pieces of metal and use them to reflect the light back towards the entryway. You get bonus points if you can do that near a decent-sized hole in the ceiling. Keep your ears open for the team I'll have upstairs. They'll have different vantage points and may be able to help you with the placement of the lanterns."

I pointed to another pair of guards. "You two go downstairs and confiscate at least half of the lanterns they've got down there in the tunnel. Leave enough that they can walk without tripping over anything, but not so much that everybody's comfortable. Then work your way back up here and see where you can legitimately remove a lantern in the basement without making it so the rest of our people that are still working their way here from the headquarters building can't get safely down to the tunnels. We're going to need all the light up here we can manage."

I waited until the two groups I'd detached headed out and then pointed at the rest of the armed men Jax had provided me. "As for the rest of you, go ahead and get upstairs and start scouting out firing positions. Remember that our enemies are going to probably have two ways of seeing in the dark. One of those is the ability to see the heat coming off of your bodies, so you're going to want to be careful not to stay in any one spot for long enough that your body heat will bleed through the floor or you'll have them shooting at you from below when you least expect it."

As my last group of men turned to go, I remembered one last thing. "Oh, yeah, you're also going to want to keep an eye out for presents from me once you're up there."

THE DESTROYER

Once all of the armed guards had been deployed, I stood there for a moment watching the stream of humanity work its way past me. Our initial group of four hundred had been joined by additional waves of noncombatants as Jax's men continued to round up everyone from farmers and textile workers to foundry technicians and power plant workers. As they walked past I was reminded of a comment Brennan had once made that the hardest task ahead of him when he'd set out to rebuild a decent technology base here in the city had been getting enough people trained up and using the right mindset.

Tyrell and Jax were about to blow up tens of thousands of people-hours and an almost inconceivable investment in materials, but Brennan had been right. Everything that was about to be destroyed—the headquarters building and the bore—could be replaced in just a year or two if I could find a way to save the massive investment in human capital that was trudging past me.

Alexander had always known exactly what he was doing. He'd used firebombs on the cities for a century and a half because he'd known that the best way to make sure he never faced legitimate opposition outside of the enclave was to keep the people who lived inside the cities from ever passing on anything that they learned to their neighbors and children.

I could've stayed there watching Brennan's people walk past me for hours, but that wouldn't help them survive what was coming. I forced myself to walk against the flow, retracing my earlier steps until I'd managed to make it back outside of the building. Along the way I gave the team that was setting out lanterns orders to head up to the second floor once they were done.

I was surprised at just how much I remembered of my surroundings on my way back out. I'd figured that I was going to have to follow the flow of people coming the other direction in order to get out of the building, but instead I found myself slotting each turn and dead end into a complex three-dimensional map inside my mind.

By the time I was out where I could see the setting sun, I'd not only noted the locations of each of the lanterns that had been placed on the ground floor, I'd also started calculating alternate routes through the wreckage and decaying interior walls. It was possible I'd be able to use that to draw the ants off in the wrong direction before circling back around to ambush them again.

Of course that only worked if it wasn't immediately obvious which way we'd gone as a result of the better part of the thousand feet having traveled that way already today. I grabbed a pair of men from the last set of noncombatants who walked past me and asked them to do what they could to obscure the path they were taking, and then there was nothing to do but check my weapon over one final time and wait.

THE DESTROYER

It was surprisingly peaceful out there, standing in front of the building where I'd almost died just a few days before. I was fully aware that the odds favored me dying within the next hour or two, but my only regret in that moment was that I couldn't see all the way to the headquarters building. Brennan and Tyrell had dismantled several buildings in the center of the compound to provide themselves with building materials, but there were enough structures remaining between me and the empty field where the Citizen-President was going to land his troops that I wasn't going to be able to see Jax and Tyrell making their final preparations. I wasn't going to get that one final glimpse of Brennan that I found myself hungering for.

At some point while I'd been inside the building, Jax had given the order for the rest of our people to fall back from the wall. I knew it was dangerous to stand out in plain sight given that the enforcers outside our walls were currently working themselves up trying to climb over the last of our fixed defenses, but I couldn't bring myself to head back inside just yet. I wanted to drink in the last of the sunlight for as long as I could.

I patted the transmitter in my pocket and wondered again if there was something I could be doing with it that would give Brennan a better chance of making it out of this alive. I was still running through possible scenarios when I saw the first of the rods descending out of the sky.

I'd read all of the available literature on the mobile command centers before I'd left the enclave. It hadn't been something that had been expected of me, but I'd figured it just made sense to pack as much information inside of my head as possible while I still had access to it.

That meant that I knew the tungsten rods that were the command center's primary armament weren't actually just dropped straight down on their targets. It was certainly possible for the command center to deploy a significant volley doing exactly that, but that required massive helium-filled airships to be directly over whatever it was they wanted to destroy.

Instead, standard operating procedure was to shoot the majority of their attacks out horizontally from the weapons platform using weak charges to provide sufficient separation from the command center to target areas outward in radius from the command center itself. The rods had rudimentary fins to make sure they didn't tumble as they descended, and to improve the accuracy with which the ant gunners could deploy their deadly payloads.

I'd read all about the flat arcs that the rods traveled through during their first few seconds of flight, and even what they looked like as they struck the ground, but none of that prepared me for being so close to Ground Zero during an actual attack.

THE DESTROYER

One moment the sky was clear, and then in the next it was full of silver and orange slivers of metal that were moving so fast that they appeared to my eyes to be many times as long as they actually were. I had only a split second between when I first registered the appearance of the rods and the first impact. Even with my nanite-given speed it wasn't enough time to make it under a doorway in case the resulting shockwaves started to bring the building down behind me.

It was like some vengeful, invisible god had taken a giant donut-shaped hammer and slammed it into the earth. A massive tectonic shockwave knocked me off of my feet a fraction of a second before a giant plume of dust shot inward from the impact sites, and I was suddenly grateful that the building behind me was blocking the worst of the man-made storm's fury as pieces of shrapnel shot across the compound wherever they could find a gap between buildings.

I could only imagine how terrifying the attack had been to the enforcers who'd been preparing to attack the compound. Everyone immediately outside of Brennan's territory had died without ever realizing they were under attack, but anyone between the compound walls and the outer edge of Brennan's territory had to be reeling in shock. I'd known what to expect before the attack landed—had even been watching for the attack for the last several minutes—and I was still having a hard time wrapping my mind around what had just happened. The dust in the air was already too thick for me to see the follow-up ring of strikes, but nothing could disguise the impact as they landed in an ever-expanding ring outward from the original set of impacts.

Immediately after the first set of strikes landed I would've said that nothing could make me able to ignore that kind of destruction, but as three more terrifying salvos of tungsten rods destroyed large sections of the city, I found out I was wrong. I couldn't ignore the effects of the strikes, not when they were capable of knocking me off my feet, but I was able to mentally separate myself from what was happening.

I'd survived the first ring of impacts, which meant that it was unlikely I was going to be taken out by a stray impact. That meant I was free to start worrying about other concerns, and I turned back toward the center of the compound.

It was almost as though Jax and Tyrell were reading my mind. A second later two sizable explosions announced the death of the first significant non-ant construction projects built in the last hundred years.

The garbage in the air was much too thick for me to get any kind of real idea as to the result of Jax's explosive charges, but I looked up in time to see the sky light up with faint blue pillars of fire as the ant dropship fired off its main thrusters. There was no longer any reason to stand outside of the building where a squad of enforcers might stumble over me.

I turned around and walked back inside to wait for the arrival of several hundred heavily armed troops who doubtlessly had orders to kill everyone but Brennan.

Tyrell hadn't been able to provide me with much usable information with regards to my capabilities, and I'd been somewhat distracted up until the strikes had started landing, so I hadn't been running through the different selections that my neural computer was eagerly offering me, but that all changed once I made it inside and sat down in one of my previously identified ambush sites.

As long as I was committed to this course of action it only made sense to put my time to the best use possible.

I sat there in the near-darkness, with dust so thick in the air that I could taste it, and started running through the menu options for my eyes. There were a surprising number of modifications that my neural computer was already prepped to make to those particular organs, so it took me some time to find what I'd been hoping for, but I couldn't help but grin when my vision flickered and then took on a red overlay that I was pretty sure corresponded to the infrared spectrum. That menu had a hot, almost electric feel to it, and it was exactly what I'd been hoping for.

That one change would mean that I had a chance of still being effective once the ants progressed past the lanterns we'd stationed on the first floor, and that was worth nearly as much as the increased speed and strength I'd been desperately hoping for when I'd first come up with my impossible plan.

It was nearly too much to hope that the upgraded version of my nanites was capable of another game-changing trick, but that didn't stop me from continuing to work my way through the invisible list of menus.

Even before I heard the crack of a smaller-caliber, faster-moving round than what Brennan had settled on for his rifles, I knew I was running out of time, but I was still surprised that the ants had already arrived on the southern border of the compound.

I had no illusions about who was ultimately in charge of the force that had been sent into the city to exterminate us. The Citizen-President was doubtlessly calling all of the shots either from the command center itself or via satellite uplink from the administration building, but whoever he had running things on the ground was better than I'd been expecting. They obviously knew the significance of the headquarters building being destroyed and had come prepared with a contingency plan to get their people headed in my direction.

That didn't bode well for my continued survival, but I found myself oddly unconcerned by my impending death. I would do my best to survive, or barring that to take as many of Alexander's sadistic troops with me as I could, but the odds against me were bad enough that it didn't matter all that much whether I was up against a commander who was the reincarnation of Napoleon or one who was a complete idiot.

Either way I was almost guaranteed not to survive.

Unlike the enforcers, who the ants seemed to be picking off from well outside of visible range for anyone not wearing the Society's standard-issue compact low-light/thermal goggles, I still had a few moments before my part of the action was going to start up, but my chance opportunity to experiment with the rest of my new capabilities had nearly come to an end.

I gritted my teeth and moved on from the last of the selections offered when I focused on the core of my body to the first of the options brought up by thinking about my skin. The first one felt like having sandpaper run across my tongue, and I got the sense that all available nanites were rushing outwards to my skin. It seemed like I could focus the protocol, which was interesting, but which probably meant that it wasn't what I was looking for.

I pushed the nanites into the skin of my right hand, and almost immediately felt the difference in the sensations coming from that area. My skin felt deadened, and when I touched it with my other hand it felt thicker and much less supple. My best bet was that the protocol had just provided me with skin that was capable of turning the point of a knife, but that wasn't going to save me—not when I was up against rifle-fire that could strike any part of my body.

The shots from outside of the building had died down, and it was quiet enough now that I was able to hear the first squad of ants enter the building. I was out of time—my troops would start shooting as soon as the ants made it close enough to one of the lanterns to be seen.

I desperately wanted to move forward and join the fight that was about to commence, but I already knew how things were going to play out there. If my nanites couldn't do what I needed them to do, then we were all going to die, and my joining sooner rather than later would only stretch things out for a few more minutes at best.

I cursed myself for not thinking things through more carefully back when I'd come up with my hare-brained scheme. I'd had Tyrell there in front of me. If I'd stopped to think about the fact that we'd be fighting in the dark against a foe who would be able to see us regardless of the conditions, then I could have asked much more specific questions about my capabilities and actually gotten something useful out of him.

I selected yet another protocol, one that tasted like a furry blanket and smelled like hot metal. That was promising, but even as I forced my nanites—which had started spreading back out to the rest of my body as soon as I'd deactivated the armor-skin protocol—back into my right hand, I heard the first wave of gunshots.

These were heavier, slower rounds, which meant that my guys had just opened up on the first group of ants from above. I looked towards the shooting just in time to see several hotspots in the ceiling disintegrate from the weight of fire directed upwards from the ants in response to the attack.

There was no way of knowing if my men had moved before they'd started firing, but if they hadn't, several of them had just been killed. The shooting from both above and below had decreased, which was a clear signal that we'd managed to take down most of their advance squad—I could only hope that my guys were just being smart and spreading out so that they could pick their shots. We couldn't afford to lose so many people in the first exchange.

I looked back down at my right hand, and was rewarded with a clear temperature difference between it and the rest of my body. Jackpot. My hope had been right, the nanites had some way of turning my skin into a much better insulator—the only question was whether they could do that to my entire body well enough to let me drop out of sight on the infrared wavelength. That and how long it was going to take for my body to cool down to the ambient temperature.

As badly as I wanted to stay out of the firefight until after my skin had stopped radiating heat, I couldn't. I tucked my rifle tight against my chest and started through the wreckage in the direction of the advance team.

By the time I arrived, it looked like there were only two ant soldiers left, and one of them was trying to provide covering fire so his companion could get around far enough to have a shot at the lantern. I'd been holding my hands up against the front and back sights of my rifle, an effort to warm them up so that I would be able to see them well enough to actually hit what I was aiming for, so it was the simplest thing in the world to put three shots into each of the two soldiers my men had pinned down.

Any urge to celebrate was blown away by the fact that even over the slight ringing in my ears I could hear another batch of soldiers entering the building. There wasn't time for anything but making sure that my people would have the ability to continue to contribute to the fight even after the lanterns were all gone.

"It's me, hold your fire for a second!"

THE DESTROYER

Without even waiting for an acknowledgment from my men, I hurried over to the soldiers' already cooling bodies and started collecting their goggles. Even working as quickly as I could, the next squad of soldiers was getting uncomfortably close by the time I started away from the ambush site.

I moved as quickly as I could through the warren of twisted metal, mind spinning frantically. It was tempting to tell my men to fall back to the next ambush site. They weren't going to be able to take the next group of soldiers by surprise like they'd done the first time around. The ants were going to be watching the roof, which meant I was going to lose more men, but that was going to be the case even if they waited for our enemies to get to the second lantern before attacking.

They were just going to have to do the best they could. I, on the other hand, needed to find something that would shield me from the ants while I climbed up to the ceiling. My entire plan would unravel pretty quickly if I got shot while dangling in midair, and even the dust that was providing a nice temperature gradient compared to the metal littering the floor would only do so much to hide my thermal signature.

Even as I had the thought, I looked down at my arms and was pleased to see that they were only a little hotter than the dust that still filled the air. I was nearly to the point of being able to implement the next stage of my plan. I used the three-dimensional map in my mind to find a spot with walls on two sides and a likely pile of scrap metal that I thought would serve my purpose.

I wasn't moving as quickly as I would've liked, but I couldn't afford to run into something with sufficient force to cut me. That would ruin my thermal camouflage in very short order.

I wasn't exerting myself very heavily, so I was surprised to see just how hot the air was every time I breathed out. About the same time, I realized that my core temperature seemed to be climbing. That made a lot of sense given that the protocol I was running had to be stopping my body's normal waste heat from exiting out through my skin like it otherwise would have.

If my suspicions were correct that meant my breath was only going to get hotter in step with everything else currently behind the thermal camouflage. That could be a problem on several levels. I was going to have to be very careful with my breathing once I got close to the bad guys, and it was possible that too high a level of exertion for too long would cause my body to start shutting down despite everything my nanites could do.

There was nothing I could do about that problem right then, so I focused on climbing up the pile of jagged metal I was hoping would get me high enough that I wouldn't break the night vision goggles as I tossed them up onto the second floor. A few seconds later I tossed all six of the goggles through a hole in the ceiling and cupped my hands to my mouth to make it harder for the ants to figure out where my voice was coming from.

"Special delivery for Brennan's people; put those on and start looking for alternative ambush sites."

I waited for an acknowledgment from whoever happened to be closest to my location and then jumped back to the ground. I was going to have to leave my rifle behind at some point once the barrel got hot enough to show up on thermal imaging, but not before I managed to get in at least one good attack. I started working my way back towards the teams I could hear coming in through the front of the building, but before I could take more than a few steps one of the ants fired a shot into the ceiling and my people responded with a hurricane of fire that tore the ants to pieces.

Apparently the first team hadn't managed to get an understandable report back as to what had happened to them, but the new teams were close enough to see what happened to the point group, and they were every bit as well-trained as I'd known they would be. Someone from the team on the left launched a grenade at the lantern, and a second later it went off and that part of the building was plunged into darkness. I wanted to yell out for my people to scatter before the ants took them all out with their rifle-mounted grenade launchers, but I knew it was too late for any warning I could give to make a difference. All I could hope was that they were smart enough to start falling back as soon as the light died.

A few seconds later five grenades went off in quick succession as the ants did their best to take my forward ambush team out despite not being able to see them. It was exactly according to protocol, and I should've seen it coming, but I was simply too inexperienced to be leading such a large group of men into battle. I was having to figure everything out on the fly, and not doing a very good job of it.

I forced my regret over not having given my people more extensive orders back into a corner of my mind and closed it behind a steel door. There would be time enough to mourn my losses if I survived the battle, and letting emotions affect me right now would just result in more of my people dying before they needed to.

Even as I'd been struggling to deal with my emotions, I'd continued moving forward and I was now less than ten yards away from the group that had just avenged their fellows. There was no way to use my rifle's sights for what I was about to do, but with any luck I was close enough that it wouldn't matter. I flipped the selector on my rifle to full auto, and raked one long, continuous burst of fire across the team of soldiers.

As soon as the slide on my rifle locked back in the empty position, I threw my weapon away from me with all of the force I could manage considering the bulk of my nanites were focused on modifying my vision and keeping my heat signature under control. I risked a quick breath as I jumped in the other direction, just ahead of the shockwave from a trio of rifle-launched grenades.

I'd managed to put enough distance between me and Ground Zero to avoid anything more than a scratch, but I knew I wasn't going to be able to repeat that kind of ambush anytime soon. It was going to have to come down to blade work.

As tempting as it was to take out the lead group, I knew that would be a mistake. Instead, I slipped over to the site of the second ambush and liberated half a dozen more goggles before heading deeper into the enemy's section of the building.

It had been anybody's guess as to whether the bad guys were going to use a smaller group of mutually supporting squads to try to hunt my men down, or if they would flood the building. There were arguments for both courses of action, but I'd been hoping for the first option because it would even our odds dramatically.

Apparently I'd been right in thinking that the ant commander would be confident that his men would have no problem slaughtering several times their own number in enemies. So far he or she seemed to be sticking with a smaller footprint in order to reduce the risk of friendly fire casualties. That worked to my advantage.

Two more squads had entered the building shortly after I'd slaughtered the squad that had launched those grenades at my men, and they were my current target. My skin hadn't cooled down all the way to the ambient temperature by that point, but it was getting close.

I stayed low in the hopes that my lower temperature gradient would combine with my silhouette being broken up to make the ant soldiers not classify me as a threat. Moving through all of the garbage and scrap metal without making a ton of noise was the most difficult part of my undertaking, but controlling my breathing was a close second.

As I moved past the sole remaining advance squad, I tried to time my breathing so that I was exhaling down close to the ground and only when I had something between them and me to at least partially obscure the plume of hot air leaving my mouth. It was difficult, but I managed it well enough to get past the point squad without any of them identifying me as something they needed to be worried about.

I was only twenty or thirty yards away from the advance squad when a group of my men tried for another ambush. A couple of ricochets howled by within just a few feet of me, but I was too busy being proud to pay much attention to how much worse things could have turned out for me if they'd begun firing even just a few seconds sooner.

THE DESTROYER

Not every ant soldier carried a weapon with the barrel-mounted grenade launcher, and my men seemed to have figured that out and correctly identified the two soldiers from the squad who were. I looked back just in time to see four of the soldiers drop in the opening barrage, and based on the fact that the return fire only consisted of standard rifle rounds, my guys had managed to take out the grenadiers in the opening salvo.

I spotted a hole in the ceiling just in front of me and paused to throw the night vision goggles I'd collected up on to the second floor. There was a chance that the goggles would take too much damage from being thrown, but their electronics tended to be fairly robust, and the goggles hadn't been doing anybody any good buckled to the side of my vest.

I could hear more commotion outside the building as additional squads were prepping to be sent in, and then a series of deep thumps that I was pretty sure were grappling hooks designed to get a squad or two up on the second floor where they could start suppressing the teams I had running around up there.

Once again, there wasn't much I could do but hope that Jax had trained this crew well enough for them to hold their own against men who were much better equipped than they were, and that they would fall back to the stairwell before the lanterns were all shot out. It would be even more of a tragedy to lose half of my shooters because they'd fallen through holes in the floor.

I was within less than a dozen yards now of the squad that I was targeting. I took a couple of deep breaths, being careful to disguise the waste heat coming out of my mouth, and then held my breath as I started forward. The squad was moving in a rough oblong shape so that they could keep rifles pointed in every direction in the hopes that we wouldn't be able to take them by surprise like we'd done their fellows.

I waited until all but the last soldier had walked past my position, and then stood and shoved my combat knife into his chest. I'd spent the last couple of minutes considering the best way to eliminate an entire squad by myself, and had decided against trying to keep my first victim quiet. Instead I was going to rely on speed and the shock of having an attacker show up right in their midst to keep me alive.

As the rear soldier started to fall, I ripped his combat knife free of the sheath where he'd fastened it on his bulletproof vest, and spun around so I could charge up the center of the squad's formation. I could never have used two weapons at the same time effectively in combat against someone who was as fast as I was and able to see me coming, but under these circumstances it was remarkably easy to cut through the renal arteries of both of the next two soldiers before they'd even realized that the last man in the squad had been attacked.

The knife I'd stolen was standard-issue, which meant that it was almost identical to the ones I'd practiced throwing when I'd been back at the enclave. It wasn't an ideal throwing weapon—especially not when throwing from my left hand—but I still managed to sink my second knife into the neck of the squad's point man.

The result was everything I could've hoped. I was now down a weapon, but rather than a clear pattern of attack moving from the back of the squad forward, I'd just created the illusion that the soldiers were under attack from multiple directions.

The next two soldiers fell in quick succession, but the last two reacted with all of the speed they could squeeze out of their nanite-infused muscles. They moved to put their backs to each other, but I got there just in time to grab the barrel of the guy on the right and spin it around so that the three-round burst that had been meant for me killed the second-to-last member of the squad.

I dropped the last member and took off at a run at right angles to the next closest squad, pausing only to pick up one of the rifles with a grenade launcher mounted to the barrel. Despite my reckless pace, I still almost didn't make it out far enough before grenadiers from other squads blanketed their fallen comrades' position with bursts of deadly shrapnel.

I was far enough away that most of the force of the blast had dissipated by the time it reached me, but I hadn't put enough distance behind me to escape completely unscathed. I felt searing pain in my left leg as a piece of shrapnel went clear through my thigh. That was no good—it was going to make me slower and leave a telltale splotch of heat around the wound that would allow my enemies to track my movements, but there wasn't anything to be done about it. I was just going to have to try to compensate.

The next phase of my plan had been only half formed when I'd grabbed the grenade launcher, and even now I wasn't sure this was the right escalation to pursue, but I had to do something soon to force the ants to fall back or else we were all going to get overrun—my special advantages notwithstanding. It was more than just my wound, my insides were still heating up faster than panting could cool me off. I felt like I was going to spontaneously combust at any moment, and shifting the protocol so that my feet were bleeding off some of the excess body heat wasn't making enough of a difference to allow me to continue functioning indefinitely.

The last high-altitude strike had been long enough in the past that some of the dust was starting to settle out of the air. Visibility still wasn't anything that could be called good, but I had no problem seeing all four squads currently inside the building on my level.

THE DESTROYER

I moved over so I was positioned behind one of the few load-bearing walls in the building and took a deep breath. The wall wasn't going to do much to stop hyper-velocity shrapnel, but it might allow me to hide the heat signature of the grenade launcher quickly enough after I started firing to allow me to escape the worst of the retaliation I was expecting.

Standard-issue barrel-mounted grenade launchers had a clip of eight grenades, and a cycle time of just over two seconds to launch all eight grenades. Cycle time figures like that were usually misleading. No normal human could hope to shoot off eight aimed shots at separate targets in that much time, but I relaxed my chameleon protocol slightly and sped up my nervous system with all of the nanites that freed up before I pulled the trigger.

I managed to get all eight shots off in just under three seconds and then dropped my commandeered rifle so I could turn and run.

Up until now the ants had maintained remarkable vocal discipline, but as the first of my grenades went off a chorus of screams was clearly audible over the sporadic rifle fire being exchanged on the second floor.

A fraction of a second after the first two grenades went off, wreaking havoc in the first squad, two more explosions signaled the arrival of my second salvo. I'd started with the most distant squad and walked my fire sequentially towards the closest squad, and the last six explosions were so close together they sounded almost like one rolling peal of thunder.

I almost thought that I'd managed to escape any kind of counter fire, but somebody must have seen the heat plume from the first of my grenades and gotten a shot off before my attack had arrived. This time I hadn't had a chance to make it quite as far away from the blast site, and took shrapnel in three places across my back and left arm.

It probably would've been worse if not for the sheltering presence of the wall. Contrary to my expectations, I heard several of the fragments of shrapnel ricochet off of the metal support beams running up and down inside of what was left of the sheet rock.

I hit the ground in a roll and winced as something on the ground sliced into my left shoulder. The initial blast of hot, dust-filled air from the bombardment had long since been replaced by cooler air and I was starting to see less and less of a temperature difference between the floor and the wreckage all around me.

I shut down most of the extra speed enhancement and split the nanites that freed up between patching my wounds and strengthening the chameleon protocol that was the only thing that had kept me alive so far. Their grenade had destroyed big sections of the sheet rock I'd been using to obscure my silhouette, so rather than rolling to my feet and continuing to run, I stayed down on my hands and knees and did a quick crawl laterally away from what was left of my wall. Despite the danger, I popped my head up far enough to confirm that there wasn't anybody still standing from any of the four squads I'd just attacked.

I debated my options for a split second and then abandoned my cover so I could run towards one of the few places I thought would give me a chance of making it up onto the second floor without detouring all the way back to the stairwell. It was a risk if the ants had thought to position snipers just outside of the building looking in, but my heat signature had already started to dissipate again and I was reasonably sure that they wouldn't register me as the threat that had just killed several dozen of their comrades.

My destination was a corroded I-beam that had come loose from the superstructure of the building and dropped so that the free end was resting on the first floor. There was a very real chance that the end still attached up on the second floor was nearly as corroded as the one that had already broken free, but I hit the bottom end of the I-beam at a run without giving myself a chance to worry about what would happen if the beam came loose underneath me while I was still only halfway up.

I'd decided to move up to the second floor out of nothing more than a desire to help what was left of my men, but once I arrived at my destination I realized that I was unarmed save for my combat knife.

Looking around at the volume of fire pouring in from the north side of the building, I was suddenly less optimistic about my ability to make any kind of difference in the fight on the second floor. It looked like the ants had several teams inside the building now. They'd taken cover behind objects with a chance of stopping a bullet, which meant I would have to cross a killing field with bullets zipping back and forth in either direction if I wanted to get close enough to start executing soldiers.

Under those kinds of circumstances even being the next best thing to invisible was probably not going to be enough to save me from being shot, so I started to revise my plan. I had just started working my way towards a group of rapidly cooling bodies in the hopes of arming myself with one of our heavier rifles when I heard the distinctive deep cough of multiple grenade launchers go off below me on the first floor.

It was a logical escalation for the ants' commander to have ordered, and I should've seen it coming, but I didn't. I threw myself towards the nearest piece of wreckage that had a chance of stopping the explosion heading my way and prayed that I also happened to be lying directly above one of the massive I-beams that provided the bulk of the structural support for the floor underneath me.

THE DESTROYER

"Take cover! Incoming gr—"

I hadn't even managed to get all of my warning out before the first floor turned into one massive, multi-pointed ball of fire. The entire building shook from the force of the explosions, but that was a secondary concern in light of the storm of shrapnel I could hear ricocheting off of beams in the process of turning everything less sturdy into scraps.

I'd been right to worry about the structural integrity of the floor. A significant chunk of the shrapnel was being shot upwards and I could hear it tearing through big sections of the floor. Before I could even ascertain whether I'd been hit from the ground-floor barrage of grenades, the ants on the second floor cut loose with a similar—if smaller—salvo of grenades.

This time the attack was designed less to kill an invisible, unstoppable adversary, and more focused on keeping my men pinned down in the three different locations from which they'd been returning fire at the ants. That meant most of the grenades were impacting quite a ways away from me, which was the only thing that saved me from being perforated in a hundred places.

My men weren't as lucky, and their screams were even more disconcerting than the screams of my enemies had been. I cupped my hands around my mouth once again to throw off anyone trying to pinpoint me by the sound of my voice.

"Fall back to the stairwell. We can't win up here."

As soon as the words left my mouth I rolled across the floor and let myself fall through a hole leading down to the ground floor. I caught myself on the edge at the last second to arrest my fall and then let myself drop the rest of the way, hoping the entire time that I wasn't about to land on some jagged shard of metal that was capable of cutting me in half.

I hit the ground with my knees bent, completely invisible to anyone still operating solely via infrared. We only had seconds until the ants on the second floor would be radioing my orders back to their commander, and I needed to make what little time I had left count.

I hurried over to the closest group of dead ant soldiers and picked up both grenade launchers, six sets of night vision goggles, and a double handful of magazines full of rifle ammunition. I had no illusions as to my ability to stage another ambush on the ground floor, but it was entirely possible that we were going to need grenades of our own.

There was one more ambush site on the way back to the stairwell, and I headed that direction hoping that I'd be able to pick up two more rifles before the ants made another sortie into the building. I had just arrived when the clatter of booted feet moving through the scrap metal on the floor brought me around.

THE DESTROYER

This time they weren't coming in black, solely dependent upon their infrared goggles. They had the lights on the rifles turned on, which probably meant they were using the lowlight option on their goggles, but I didn't dare drop my chameleon protocol. There was simply too much chance that one or more of the soldiers in each squad was still using the infrared mode to keep their bases covered.

I found the two grenade launchers from the first squad I'd ambushed after only a few seconds of searching and slung both of them over my right shoulder. I was shaking as I grabbed four more goggles off the wreckage that had been living, breathing human beings just a short time ago.

It was tempting to just grab more ammo and go. Based on the number of feet I'd heard moving out after I'd ordered the retreat, I was starting to doubt that I had enough surviving guardsmen to justify stopping to collect more sets of goggles, but a man without goggles at this point was as good as dead anyway. Our best bet for holding off the ants was to make sure as many of my surviving men as possible were actually going to be in a position to fight.

I finished looping the goggles through the sling on one of the rifles, reattached the sling and then moved out at a pace that was nothing short of reckless. My mind was whirling, furiously trying to come up with a location that would provide some degree of cover from the massed grenade fire I was pretty sure would be headed my way.

On both my way into the building and when I'd come back out after reaching the tunnels, I'd been focused primarily on evaluating the terrain from the standpoint of dealing with rifle fire, and I was having a hard time re-rendering my three-dimensional map in such a way as to allow me to think in terms of area effect weapons.

Under other circumstances I probably would've just kept running until I made it to the stairwell, but any of my men who were retreating without the aid of the night vision goggles I'd stolen from the ants were going to be moving a lot more slowly than I was. I needed to buy them some time.

I was nearly to the stairwell in the center of the building by the time that I decided I was going to have to just improvise. There was a metal door lying on its side a couple dozen yards away from my destination, and it was going to have to do.

I left both my infrared vision and my chameleon protocols in place, but I rerouted the rest of my available nanites out to my skin in an effort to strengthen it in the hopes it would turn some of the shrapnel if my plan went disastrously awry.

It was even easier to pick out the approaching squads of soldiers now that they were all using the lights mounted to their rifles, and I once again snugged the model of rifle I'd originally trained with up tight against my shoulder and shot off a full clip of grenades, moving laterally across three groups, before lunging to the right and hopping over the metal door that I was hoping would save me from the return fire I could already hear headed my way.

It was a strategy that relied on the competence of my enemies rather than upon their incompetence for once. If they all landed their grenades within a few feet of where my muzzle flash had been, then the steel door would be between me and the grenades when they went off. Even if they landed their grenades to the right of where they were aiming at, I should be okay. If, however, any of them lobbed a grenade to the left, there was a decent chance that I'd find myself sandwiched between the door and a buzz saw of lethal shrapnel.

Even before I managed to finish crouching down behind the door, my grenades went off in rapid succession like giant, deadly firecrackers. Half a second later the return fire from the ants arrived and the side of the door closest to me bulged from the effort of trying to contain such an incredible hail of sharp-edged metal.

The door struck me with enough force to knock me onto my side as the ricochets from fragments that had cleared the door and then bounced back in my direction arrived. I took a couple of smaller strikes to my leg and a bigger piece that went all the way through the left side of my chest just below the bottom of my lung.

I rolled back to my knees just in time to see lights approaching from the east. Whoever was in charge of the other side had finally decided to send in all of his forces at once. The new squads had stepped into the building too late to see me decimate the three squads that had been my latest victims, but there was nothing to say that they wouldn't decide to lob a couple grenades my direction anyway. It was time to fall back.

I made it to the stairwell as the clatter of booted feet heralded the arrival of my remaining men. "Don't shoot, it's me."

"What do you want us to do, Skye? You've gotten us this far against all odds, I'm excited to see what else you've got up your sleeve."

I could hear the relief in the voice of the guy who'd asked the question, and it just reinforced the fact that everyone was depending on me to come up with some kind of miracle that would let us get out of there alive. I didn't have the heart to tell him that we had already done far better than I'd been expecting.

"I scavenged more goggles off of some of the soldiers I took out down here, but we've got groups headed in from at least two or three sides now. It looks like they're going to just make one concerted effort to take us out. How far behind are the ones chasing you?"

THE DESTROYER

Of the eight guards who'd survived this long, four of them already had goggles and I found myself wishing that I'd substituted body armor for at least some of the goggles dangling from my sling. Still, the expressions of relief on the faces of the four men who'd been essentially operating blind helped remove some of the sting from my mistake.

"Maybe thirty seconds. We all fired off a full magazine of ammo at them right before diving into the stairwell. We figured the concrete ought to withstand however many of those grenades they wanted to shoot at us."

I nodded as the last of my men got their goggles into place. "Good job. This level is a loss as well. We need to head downstairs and establish a perimeter around the doorway to the stairwell. The basement ceiling is in a lot better shape than the one between the first and second floor, but you're still going to want to be careful. It doesn't matter how good a cover you've got from the front if you put yourself in a spot where they can shoot you from above."

I waited to make sure that everybody understood and then led them down the stairs, at the next best thing to a run. The last thing we wanted was to be stuck inside such a small space if one of the ants got close enough to start throwing grenades at us.

I handed the rifle whose grenade launcher I'd just emptied off to one of the men for safekeeping and then handed out two of the three remaining captured rifles. We all spread out so that we were within a dozen yards of the hole down into the tunnels, arranged in an arc that would give us the ability to shoot at anybody trying to take shelter inside the stairwell.

As I was showing the second guard how to use the grenade launcher on his captured rifle, he asked me a question I should have anticipated.

"I swear we've been hitting these guys and not putting them down. How come they're so hard to kill?"

"They're wearing body armor. Brennan's rifles shoot a round that's a lot heavier than the ants were expecting to go up against, but it's not enough to always penetrate the armor and take one of them down. With the rifle you're holding, you're going to pretty much have to take them in the head or cut their legs out from underneath them to bring them down."

"Okay, that's good to know—I'll pass the word on. What about these grenades, can they penetrate the body armor?"

I shook my head. "No, but they don't typically need to. If you can drop a grenade close enough to someone, they'll take enough damage to the rest of their body that it won't matter that their torso is covered up."

I half expected the ants to send some of their drones down ahead of their men to scout what they were up against, but apparently Brennan's jammer was still working, because rather than the electronic henchmen I'd been worried about, they came down with a single team moving with all of the speed their nanite-infused muscles were capable of.

Against lesser foes that might have worked, but I was ready for them and I put a three-round burst into the neck of the lead soldier. That dropped him to the ground and slowed his companions down just enough for my men to cut the rest of the squad down before they could get far enough out of the stairwell to take cover.

My men cheered at finally managing to take out an entire squad again without losing one of their own. I was smiling just as broadly as everyone else, but I wasn't as convinced that we'd managed to completely turn the tables on the ants. My men still thought in terms of fighting enemies with capabilities no greater than their own. I'd been locked in much the same mindset up until now, but I was starting to realize just how dangerous that was. I was now making a conscious effort to overcome that shortcoming.

I debated possible courses of action for several seconds, and then picked four of my eight men and motioned for them to go down the tunnel. As long as we still had the grenades and five of us pouring fire into the stairwell, it was going to be all but impossible for the ants to overrun us—at least not as long as we still had ammunition. I waited for a second until the four I'd ordered to go down to the tunnels had disappeared from sight, and then tapped the guy closest to me on the shoulder.

"Work your way around to the side so you're not directly exposed to anybody shooting out of the stairwell, and position yourself close enough that you can hear people coming down the stairs. Give us a signal about the time you think they're hitting the bottom of the stairs and we'll lob a grenade in there."

Nearly another five minutes passed in nerve-racking silence without anything happening. I rerouted the nanites operating the chameleon protocol on the back half of my body into my nervous system in an attempt to milk every bit of speed possible out of my augmentations.

It was an important step to take, but it meant that the five minutes seemed to stretch out to more than ten. I had to keep telling myself that things weren't moving as slowly as they seemed, or I would've lost my mind waiting like that. I was sure that the ant commander was coming up with a plan he was confident I couldn't counter.

He'd come in sloppy, much sloppier than I had any right to expect given all of the contingency plans he obviously had in place, but that was before he'd realized that he had to be up against something completely outside of his realm of experience. I was confident that he didn't know I was the next step in the evolution of nanite technology, but that didn't mean that he wasn't starting to get at least some idea of my capabilities.

THE DESTROYER

The ants' military was many times the size of Brennan's force of guards—even before we'd started losing people over the last two days—but by the same stretch they had a lot more commitments, and that meant there was a definite limit to how many people could be detached for an assault like this without creating dangerous weaknesses in the forces tasked to keep control over the smuggling routes between the rest of the cities.

When the next attack came my man crouching with his ear up to the concrete structure of the stairwell was only able to give us about five seconds' warning, but that was more than enough time for me to fire two grenades directly into the door we'd propped open on our way into the basement.

I'd reacted with all of the inhuman speed my nanites were capable of granting me, but I still almost wasn't fast enough. A split second before my grenades hit their target and went off, the soldier who'd been sneaking down the stairs fired off a full magazine of eight grenades.

My grenades killed him, but the rest of my men were still trying to get shots of their own at him when his grenades went off only a few yards away from us. I'd tried to yell out a warning as I hit the deck, but none of my guys were fast enough to get all the way back under cover before the grenades went off.

One of my guys was killed instantly, another took a piece of shrapnel to his chest, but was able to scoot back out of the way so that he was under cover in case another wave of grenades came at us. At that moment I was desperately wishing I had a syringe so I could inject the guy with the chest wound, but I didn't. Even if I'd had a syringe, there was no guarantee that I could've figured out how to program my nanites to repair his body while simultaneously watching for another attack.

I waved for the uninjured guy closest to me to apply first-aid to the one with the chest wound and debated options. There was no worthwhile cover closer to the stairwell, at least not close enough to significantly change my line of sight to the stairs. The ants had no way of knowing for sure that they'd just killed one of my guys and severely wounded another, but that didn't necessarily mean that they were going to stop attacking. They'd been able to hear the grenades go off, and I was confident this particular commander would think nothing of sacrificing a few more men if it would let them get another dozen or two grenades fired off in our direction.

Despite that, with every passing second I got the feeling that that wasn't the course my opponent had decided on. I could hear a lot of movement from up on the ground floor, but nothing distinguishable enough to give me any clue as to what they had planned.

Additional long minutes trickled past with glacial slowness, but I just kept telling myself that every minute that passed put Lexis and the rest of the noncombatants a minute closer to the other end of the tunnels.

I'd just turned to check on my wounded man when a muffled series of thumps traced a square around a section of the ceiling above us, and then things happened almost too fast even for me to react to them. A massive section of the ceiling came down in a roar of overstressed metal.

I did the only thing I could. I dived towards the hole that led down into the tunnel.

For the briefest of moments I thought I wasn't going to make it, but then I cleared the edge of the hole and fell straight down as the patch of ceiling crashed downwards and sealed off the hole above me. Even with all of my unusual advantages, I'd still survived mostly out of luck.

I hit the ground, more than twenty feet below me, hard enough to break my left arm in three places. The cascade of rubble knocked loose from the lip of the hole by the sheer force of the impact when the ants blew the ground floor could have easily killed me. Some of the pieces that hit me were as big around as my head, and I was lucky to escape with nothing worse than massive bruises, a set of broken ribs, and a broken arm.

I struggled to my feet in a daze trying to understand why the ant commander would've decided to seal off his only way into the tunnel that he thought contained Brennan. It didn't make sense. I was positive that the Citizen-President had given orders for Brennan to be brought in alive if at all possible.

There was only one way to get to Brennan, or at least where they thought Brennan was, and no tactician with his stripes would knowingly collapse the entrance to the tunnel like that...unless they had just realized that the entrance they'd just collapsed wasn't the only way to get to him.

They'd collapsed the building floor not to stop us from counterattacking, but because they'd decided it was the best way to eliminate a significant chunk of Brennan's guards. If I didn't make it to the front of the group before the ants found the exit tunnel, Lexis and the rest of the noncombatants were going to get massacred.

I pulled myself to my feet, noting that my enclave-issued rifle had somehow managed to survive the fall, and then nearly passed out from the pain of all of my injuries. I was so far gone that it took me several laborious steps to figure out what was going on. Everything hurt more than it should have because unlike the last time I'd sustained major injuries, my nanites weren't free to act on their own anymore.

I released my nanites from the chameleon protocol they'd been running and re-tasked them to deaden the nerves around the injuries as they went about stabilizing the bones and knitting them back together.

I found myself wishing that I had a good idea how long it was going to take my nanites to get me back into fighting shape, but the last thing I expected was for a digital countdown to superimpose itself on my field of vision. Apparently Tyrell hadn't been kidding when he'd said that my neural computer would tailor itself to my needs.

I did some quick math trying to estimate the average ground speed of a group of men, women and children over smooth terrain and then compared it against the amount of time that I thought I'd been fighting so far and the estimate that was counting down in the upper-right corner of my vision.

It wasn't going to be fast enough unless the tunnel was a lot longer than I thought it was. Inspiration struck me a second later and I sighed in relief when I found that the flashlight mounted on the side of the barrel was still functional as well.

Releasing the nanites that had been powering my infrared vision brought the estimated time until my bones were healed down a small but noticeable amount, but it was still looking like I was going to come up a few minutes late until I realized that it might be possible to focus my nanites on my arm. I could fight through the pain of broken ribs—especially with my nanites numbing the nerves—but I couldn't reliably aim my rifle with just one hand.

I tried to order my neural computer to move some of the nanites away from my ribs and was rewarded a second later with a second countdown. The top one represented my arm and was now less than two-thirds of the original estimate while the bottom readout was indicating that my ribs were still more than two hours away from being back to normal. I could live with that.

All of that had taken less than a minute, but it had so completely consumed me that it was a surprise when I stepped around a bend in the tunnel and found myself face-to-face with the business end of four rifles.

"It's me—Skye."

The rifles came down as one. "Commander, what happened up there?"

"We had the stairwell dialed in too well, and the ants couldn't get past so they decided to drop the ceiling on us. Nobody else made it to the hole in time. I'm sorry, I don't think there's any way the rest of the team survived."

The guardsman I had just answered looked like he wanted to be sick, but he shook himself and fell in next to me as I continued down the tunnel.

"So does that mean we're safe now? I mean, the ants could probably dig us out, but do you really think that they'll spend the time?"

THE DESTROYER

A dozen different answers sprang to mind, any of which would have provided the guardsmen, a young man no older than me, with information he needed while not implicating myself, but after everything that happened over the last week I just couldn't bring myself to keep lying. I gave him the answer that was the most truthful, the one that was very possibly going to get me into trouble.

"I wish it was, but the only reason they would've sealed the tunnel like that is if they figured out where the other end comes to the surface. We're in more danger now rather than less. Now we're going to be the ones attacking a defensive position, and we're still going to be outnumbered and outgunned. Our only chance now is to get ahead of the ants and make it up out of the tunnel before they're ready for us."

I'd continued to increase my pace while talking, testing how badly it was going to jolt my damaged body for several steps before ramping it up further. By the time I'd finished answering his question, I was nearly up to the jog that was the fastest pace I could sustain without an assist from my nanites, and so far the countdown readouts had remained steady.

I was starting to feel a sliver of hope that it might be possible to get back up to the surface before the ants had a chance to dig in, and ticked my pace up the tiniest bit to my maximum sustainable speed, only to see both of the counters increase by fifty percent.

Apparently I'd just exceeded the force that my nanites were able to compensate for. I gritted my teeth, but I slowed back down so that I would still be in a position to fight when I arrived. I told myself there was still a chance that the ants would be forced to slow down if they ran into what was left of the enforcers on the south side of Brennan's territory.

The young guardsman who was still running at my side had been lost in thought while I was trying to figure out the limits of my healing ability.

"How did they figure out where the tunnel was going to end? One of those satellites up in orbit? Maybe they've got one with some way of seeing underground?"

There it was. I could either choose to deceive, like I'd done up to this point, or I could tell the truth.

"No, none of their satellites are capable of seeing through this much dirt and metal. They know where the tunnel exit is because I called them after Brennan was kidnapped. They didn't know what I was doing, but I used their satellites to find where Brennan had been taken. Apparently they asked the analyst I was talking to and he told them—that or they found a record of our conversation on their servers."

All four of my men stumbled to a stop.

"Wait, if you called them that means you're one of them."

I nodded. "I used to be. I was sent here to steal one of Brennan's inventions, but I defected. I used their resources to help me get Brennan back, and now we're leading the bulk of their troops on a wild goose chase so that they'll leave the dropship vulnerable. Hopefully that will allow Brennan, Tyrell, Jax, and the others to capture it and get out of here. This isn't Brennan's plan, it's mine."

All four of the guardsmen had their rifles up, not quite pointed at me but so close as to not make any difference. "A plan that's gotten a lot of us killed."

"Yeah, a lot of us have died, but even more of them have died. There was some stuff I didn't anticipate that I should have, but before you go thinking that I betrayed you, stop and consider how well you would've done without me. I killed what, forty or fifty of them? I didn't have to do that any more than I had to throw those goggles you're wearing up where you could get them. I've been fighting for your survival—for the survival of all of those people up ahead of us—every step of the way. If we don't survive, it won't be because I wasn't trying."

I could see the wheels turning in their heads. They wanted to trust me, but for the first time the pieces were starting to click into place. They'd known subconsciously that no normal person could do the things I'd done upstairs in that firefight. Now that they'd been forced to acknowledge their suspicions they knew that I was part of a group that had systematically killed and oppressed them since before the time of their grandparents.

Their hatred of everything related to the ants was so bone-deep that even knowing I might be their only chance to survive, still wasn't enough to counteract their distrust of me. My nanites were already moving, repositioning away from my arm and ribs so that they could speed up my reflexes, but even for me that wasn't an instantaneous process. I was getting a crash course in the dangers of forcing all of my nanites away from the standard protocol set that my neural computer had run automatically before Tyrell had upgraded me.

The guardsmen's decision balanced on the edge of a knife as several million nanites made it up to my eyes and their heat signatures suddenly blossomed inside my field of vision. I saw the finger of the guy on the right start to tighten, and knew I was out of time.

My rifle dangling from its sling, I exploded forward with all the strength my mostly human muscles were capable of, and knocked the guy on the right's muzzle to the side a split second before his weapon discharged a three round burst. The muzzle flash burned my right shoulder, but the bullets whizzed harmlessly past me as I slammed my shoulder into my first opponent's chest at the same time that I swept his leg out from underneath him.

THE DESTROYER

He hit the ground hard enough to knock the wind out of him, but I hadn't let go of his rifle and I was now strong enough to tear it out of his hands despite his best effort. I continued forward, forcing the rest of the squad to try to track my movements as I flipped my captured rifle around and then jammed the muzzle up under the throat of the next closest guy.

"Drop them. All of you drop them or I'll be forced to blow his head off."

"I thought you just said you were on our side."

I couldn't blame anyone for the bitterness in their response, but I didn't let the barrel of my gun waver at all.

"I am, but even if you're too stupid to see that, I'm still not going to let you kill me. Now put the weapons down."

All three of the remaining rifles hit the ground at the same time, and I waved the guardsmen back away from their weapons. The five of us looked at each other in silence for several seconds before I sighed. There was no way for me to pick up their weapons and still keep a gun trained on them—not with only one functioning arm.

"If I was really your enemy the smart thing would be to just shoot all four of you and then make up some lie once I caught back up with everyone else. I think we can agree the last thing an agent of the ants would do in this situation is give you back your guns. So that's what I'm going to do. Under normal circumstances I could run the four of you into the ground, or barring that I could always just make you head the other direction far enough that there was no way you'd be able to rush me before I had all of the weapons picked back up, but these aren't normal circumstances.

"My arm's broken, my ribs are fractured, and we've already wasted time that we don't have. I'm going to go do my best to get us all out of here and save Lexis and those two girls in the process. If you want to shoot me do it now and save me the effort of trying to run while my nanites piece me back together."

Chapter 10

I dropped my most-recently-captured weapon onto the ground next to the other three and then turned around and walked away without looking back. It was probably a good strategy not to run immediately so that I didn't look like I was scared of them, but the truth was that I needed a few seconds to work myself back up to something more than a walk.

I was quite simply at the end of my rope. Since Brennan had been captured two days ago I'd been forced to heal from everything from concussions and stab wounds to gunshot wounds. Nanites were capable of incredible things, but they still required time and raw materials to piece someone back together after that kind of damage.

When you added in the fact that Tyrell's injections had resulted in a massive upgrade to my internal infrastructure without supplementary injections of all of the raw materials required, it was no surprise that the organic side of my system was on its last legs. Up until now I'd been able to mask the natural effects of everything I'd been through with liberal use of my nanites to prop up all of the systems that were threatening to fail. Now that my nanites were fully tasked on simply keeping me alive while repairing my arm, all of that exhaustion was starting to leak through to my conscious mind.

My legs burned with uncleared lactic acid, but I forced myself to speed back up to a pace that had at least a slim chance of making it to the tunnel exit before the ants arrived. I could hear the guardsmen behind me moving forward. Even after they picked up their weapons there was no burst of fully automatic rifle fire to cut me in half, and after a short time they caught up to me.

"If you're so worried about everyone down here in the tunnel with us, how come you're not running faster? I've heard stories, you ants are supposed to be inhumanly fast."

"Yeah, I could leave you all in my dust, but if I did that I'd arrive at the exit with a broken arm and my ribs still messed up. This way I may arrive a couple of minutes too late, but at least when I arrive my arm should work well enough to be able to shoot this weapon. If I'm not moving quickly enough for you, feel free to run ahead without me."

I wasn't sure if they were worried about making it to the group and then not knowing what to do once they got there, or if they just didn't trust me at their backs with a loaded gun, but for whatever reason all four of them stayed with me, matching my speed as we traveled down the dim tunnels.

By the time we caught up with the rearguard, which consisted of nothing more than untrained men and women in guard uniforms who were holding inoperable rifles, it felt as though I'd been running for hours, but based on the progress the countdown timers at the top of my vision had made, it had been less than half an hour. As we got closer to the mass of people choking the tunnel, I waited for the four guards who'd been accompanying me to reveal my secret, but none of them seemed quite willing to be the first to out me.

I looked over at the guy my age and gave him an inquiring look, which just made him shrug uncomfortably. "If you're really trying to help everyone, then starting a panic is just going to make your job harder. If you're not, well, I don't suppose it really matters. If you're working for the other side we're all screwed anyway. Making sure we take you with us seems kind of petty, and it's not worth ruining your chances of saving us if you're telling the truth."

I nodded. "I appreciate you being willing to give me the benefit of the doubt. Not everybody would do that—I'm not sure I would've been able to do that a few weeks ago."

The press of bodies ahead of us had forced us to slow down to something only barely more than a walk, which was plenty frustrating considering the time constraints we were operating under, but had the added benefit of making it so we could talk at a normal volume without gasping.

The guard I'd been talking to held out his hand with a smile. "The name is Tom, by the way. As for whether you'd be able to do the same if you were in my place, that's one of those things you can never know until you're in the situation—you'll have to just trust me on that. If someone had told me that I'd be facing that kind of choice a few hours ago, I would've told him nothing could convince me to act the way I just did. Thanks, by the way, for pulling our butts out of the fire back in the building. You're right that we wouldn't have lasted ten minutes back there by ourselves."

I shook Tom's hand and returned his smile. "It's good to meet you, Tom. My name is Skye, but then you already know that. Any idea how to get us to the front of this pack sooner rather than later?"

"Sure, just a sec." Tom cupped his hands to his face and cut loose with a bellow that seemed like it should've come out of a much larger person. "Everybody stop walking and shift to the right! We need to get Skye to the front of the procession. Now move like your lives depend on it!"

THE DESTROYER

The noncombatants were all packed into the tunnel pretty tightly, so even after they crowded in more tightly there still wasn't room for people to walk by three abreast, but there was room for Tom and me to hurry through the hole he just created in the sea of humanity before us. I kicked my pace back up to the jog that was the best my nanites could withstand while trying to finish mending my broken bones, and less than a minute later I could see empty tunnel ahead of us.

The two guards I'd detached as pathfinders both had lanterns, as did a number of other people at the front the group, so it was finally bright enough that even the lowest setting on the ant goggles I'd stolen for Tom and the others was too bright. Tom pulled his goggles off, letting them dangle freely around his throat, as he matched my pace, and I revised my estimate of his age downwards now that I could see his whole face.

I was wondering bemusedly how we'd gotten to this point. It seemed incredible that I'd found myself in a situation where someone as young as me was in charge of the safety of nearly a thousand men, women and children, many of whom were several times as old as I was. The idea that someone even younger than me was speaking for most of my remaining guardsmen was nothing short of ludicrous.

I forced myself back into the present and pointed for one of my pathfinders to remain with the noncombatants while the other one hurried to join Tom and the rest of us. I'd considered bringing both of them along, but it seemed only prudent to make sure that the men and women who'd been tasked with maintaining order in such a large group had at least one person with a firearm to back them up if things got dicey for some reason.

As we finally got far enough ahead that the civilians wouldn't be able to hear our conversation, Tom cleared his throat. "Why are you doing this, Skye? Is it because of Brennan? I mean, we've all seen the way you look at him, and the way he looks at you..."

The way Tom trailed off there at the end of his question made it obvious he was nearly as uncomfortable with the topic as I was, but I figured I owed him an answer.

"Honestly, I'm not a hundred percent sure from one moment to the next how I got here. Brennan is definitely a factor, but he's not the only reason. You're right that I'm interested in him, but if that's all this was I would probably be back with him, Tyrell, and Jax trying to take over the dropship right about now."

"If it's not just because of him, then why?"

"It's partly because I believe in the dream that brought all of you together. I didn't know that until I arrived here, but there's something incredible about seeing hundreds of people working together to create something bigger than themselves. You don't see that where I'm from. There's more to it though. I guess maybe I grew up hearing about how everyone owes everybody else our best effort and it sank in more than I realized. Leaving all of you to face this by yourselves would be the worst kind of selfishness. I couldn't bring myself to do that, not now that I know so many of you by name."

Tom was silent for several seconds as he considered my words. "It's not usually like this, you know. I snuck into Brennan's territory from one of the territories to the north of here. Things were a lot different where I grew up. Mostly we just spent a lot of time being scared and killing each other."

I nodded. "Yeah, I know. I guess we both come from somewhere different enough from Brennan's territory to be able to appreciate what we found when we got here."

The tunnel had long since gone from being straight to meandering back and forth in a seemingly random manner. I'd been trying to keep track of the direction we'd been headed so that I would have an idea of which turnoff was most likely to lead to the exit Piter's men had used when they'd kidnapped Brennan, but apparently I hadn't been paying enough attention. When I tried to consult the same kind of three-dimensional map that my neural computer had helped create in preparation for the firefight with the ants, I came up empty.

That didn't do anything for my mood, which Tom and the rest seemed to sense as our journey progressed. We made the next twenty minutes of our trip in silence and I began worrying that our less direct path was going to result in our not being able to make it to the exit before the ants did.

I clearly remembered the analyst who'd helped me track down Brennan after we'd been ambushed using average ground speed as one of the search parameters when he'd been trying to reacquire the group after they'd disappeared to go under the barricade, but I wasn't sure that had been the case when he'd been trying to find them after they first popped back up after leaving this tunnel. More and more I was starting to realize that my assumptions regarding how long it was going to take to make it to the surface were profoundly flawed.

With each passing moment I became more and more convinced that we were going to come around a corner and run into an ambush. The longer we were in the tunnel, the less likely it was that we were going to make it to the surface, but slowing down now to make sure that we didn't blunder into an ambush would just guarantee that we wouldn't make it to the surface before the ants had a chance to find the tunnel and get dug in.

The only upside to the fact that we'd been traveling for so long was the fact that my arm was nearly healed, and once my nanites were re-tasked to my ribs it would only be a few minutes before they would be patched up as well. As big of a relief as that was, I was fairly sure it was just going to mean that I would be going to my death in tip-top shape.

We traveled for another fifteen minutes before I heard something and motioned for my men to spread out. I counted to five and then turned off the light on my rifle as the two guardsmen with lanterns moved backwards so as not to provide too much light for our enemies if that was really what I'd heard.

It took some mental fumbling to find and reactivate my thermal chameleon protocol, but I didn't bother with my thermal vision this time. The tunnel didn't have the kind of heat differentials that would allow me to pick my way over what was left of the tracks without tripping and falling.

Instead, I pulled one of the extra pairs of goggles I'd stolen off of the sling to my rifle and slipped it over my eyes. The glass was cracked, but when I turned on the power button the goggles flickered a couple of times and then settled onto the ghostly night vision mode that I'd been hoping for.

The lanterns were quite a ways back now, but they still provided just enough light for the light-gathering mode to function. I reminded myself that the scouts I was more and more certain were waiting for me just around the corner were probably using night vision mode rather than thermal imaging and then I crept forward with my right shoulder pressed up against the side of the tunnel.

I didn't like knowing that I was likely just as visible to the bad guys as they were going to be to me, but there wasn't anything I could do about it other than use my remaining nanites to juice my speed as much as I could manage and then hope that I could beat the ant soldiers to the draw.

I motioned Tom over to me and used whispers to explain my plan, and then there was nothing to do but charge around the bend in the tunnel.

I identified the trooper on the left as soon as I made it a couple of steps in. He'd wedged himself back into a crack in the wall where part of the tunnel had started to collapse in an effort to blend into his surroundings, but the muzzle flare as he fired at me was unmistakable.

My left arm still wasn't quite to a hundred percent. If I tried to punch someone with it I would probably have broken the bones in the same three spots my nanites had been working on for the last half an hour, but the repairs they'd made up to that point meant that I was able to support the weight of my rifle and even aim with a reasonable assurance that the bullets would go where I wanted them to.

I whipped my rifle around, struggling to put the glowing red dot in my enclave-made scope on the white and black silhouette that was hurling hyper-velocity lead in my direction. I'd come around the corner moving much more quickly than my enemy had expected, and his first two shots were several inches behind me, but at this range it didn't matter how fast I was, he was going to catch up to me sooner or later.

A second before I expected the third bullet to smash into me, I planted my left foot to bring myself instantly to a stop as my sights settled onto my target and I fired off a three-round burst. I'd given myself only a sixty percent chance of surviving, but relief crashed through me as the third shot slammed into the side of the tunnel just ahead of me, and my bullets tore into the ant soldier in one of the few spots where he wasn't armored.

I was pretty sure there was at least one more soldier crouched in the darkness—it seemed unlikely that the enemy commander would've sent out scouting teams comprised of only one person each—and I had a sneaking suspicion that the same trick wouldn't work a second time. Even if the second soldier hadn't been able to see me, he had to know that I'd ended up being much faster than his comrade had expected.

Now that I had confirmation that my enemies were using the night vision mode on their goggles, I released the thermal chameleon protocol and activated the skin-toughening protocol that I'd discovered earlier. I concentrated my nanites on the front half of my body, specifically my torso and head, and then nodded for Tom to execute his part of the plan.

Tom flipped his rifle to full auto and then stepped around the corner as he laid down a single long burst at waist level. I didn't actually expect Tom to hit anything with his attempt, but I was more than happy to settle for him keeping our enemy's head down.

Unfortunately Tom's inexperience was working against me this time. He was nervous enough that he didn't get far enough around the bend in the tunnel, and by the time I threw myself forward, the ant soldier had already figured out that Tom's fire was all impacting well to the left of him and he wasn't in any danger from Tom's attack.

He was already popping back up, rifle aimed directly at the spot where I'd just appeared, as I found him and tried to get the barrel of my rifle down to where I had a chance of hitting him instead of just shooting uselessly above his head. It was a race, one where I was starting from a major disadvantage, and I had only a split second before I saw fire blossom from the end of my enemy's weapon.

As I pulled the trigger on my rifle I wondered if going with a full-speed loadout rather than trying to armor myself would've been enough to let me get the first shot off, and then the first of the three-round burst slammed into me. It was like being kicked by an angry mule.

THE DESTROYER

I was slammed backwards into the wall with enough force to leave bruises all over my body, but even as I winced from the pain of being hit so hard, I realized that was actually a good thing. If my armor protocol hadn't worked then the bullets wouldn't have delivered that kind of blunt-force trauma to my body, they would have just sliced right through my flesh.

Being hit by several bullets that should've killed me instantly was every bit as disorienting as one would expect, and I was struggling to get my rifle back on target when I realized that it was taking so long precisely because the soldier's head was no longer where it had been a moment previously. My shot had landed exactly where I'd placed it, and while I was struggling to deal with the shock of having been shot, he'd been falling to the ground already dead.

I'd been lucky—much luckier than I had any right to expect—but I wasn't about to make the same mistake that I'd made earlier. I grabbed Tom's arm and turned him so he was facing the soldier I'd just killed.

"Go strip off his armor and his helmet. We're not going to leave that stuff behind. Either put it on yourself or give it to one of the other guys, and then grab his rifle and all the ammunition he's got on him. The fact that the ants have scouts down here means that they've already entered the tunnel, and I suspect we're going to need all of the ammo we can get our hands on if we're going to have any hope of shooting our way out of here."

Tom looked understandably uneasy at the prospect of stripping bloody body armor off of a dead man, but I didn't wait around to see whether he decided the prospect of being armored was more alluring than the discomfort of wearing another man's blood. I headed over to the first soldier I'd killed and started putting his body armor on over the top of my guard-issue shirt, but not until after I'd pried three flattened slugs out of my skin.

I'd donned similar armor dozens of times back in the enclave before being sent on my first and only mission, but this was the first time I'd tried to put on armor that had been sized for someone else. I struggled a little with the compression straps, but eventually got everything situated to my satisfaction and moved on to examining the weapon and ammunition that the soldier had been carrying.

I'd half hoped I would find another grenade launcher, but I wasn't surprised when that turned out not to be the case. In all reality, if the two scouts had been armed with a grenade launcher they probably would've opened fire on us while they were still hidden behind the bend in the tunnel and none of us would've survived. We'd been fortunate that the enemy commander had felt his remaining grenade launchers too valuable to waste on a scouting team, but it still left the question of how we were going to deal with the main body of men once we found them.

There was no doubt in my mind but that they still had a supply of grenades with our names on them. And I was out of ideas when it came to ways of neutralizing many times our own number on a battlefield where I couldn't hide or otherwise use terrain features to my advantage. There wasn't anything else to do but just soldier on and hope for the best.

Once I'd geared myself back up, I looked down and realized I was still holding onto the vest that Lexis had sewn for me. It was silly when you got right down to it. The vest was dirty and ragged—and now sported multiple bullet holes from hyper-velocity slugs that should've ended my life—but it was mine. Lexis had made it for me out of simple appreciation for my having saved Brennan.

I hadn't realized it at the time, but that was one of the initial, albeit tiny, turning points for me. I'd saved Brennan not because I'd been under orders to do so, or even because I'd been hoping for some kind of long-term payout like had been the case for most of my actions back in the enclave, but rather because it had felt like the right thing to do. In a lot of ways, that was the first time I'd been true to myself rather than true to what I thought was expected out of me.

I looked down at the vest for a couple more seconds and then threaded my sling through the armholes before reattaching the webbing to my rifle. Maybe I was being silly, but if I survived what I was headed into, I didn't want to have to look back and regret throwing that tiny piece of history away.

I handed the spare rifle and one of the magazines of ammo to the pathfinder, who'd ironically ended up at the back of the squad, and then, after confirming everyone else was ready to go, we headed out. We were no longer jogging now that I knew there was no hope of beating the Citizen-President's men to the tunnel entrance. Instead, we moved slowly, with our eyes peeled for any kind of booby-traps and our ears straining for anything that would indicate we were about to walk into an ambush.

I was a little surprised that we didn't run into either another set of scouts or a turnoff where the tunnel split into another direction. If it had been me in charge of the other team, I would've sent out multiple groups of scouts so that my men could split up whenever they found alternative routes that needed to be explored, but the more I thought about it the more I could see how the enemy commander had arrived at their decision.

Ant soldiers were all in constant communication with each other by way of micro transmitters implanted in their jawbones, so the commander would know as soon as his men came to any kind of crossroads. That would make it a simple matter to dispatch another squad, and if the ants had run into any kind of significant opposition from the enforcers on their way out of the compound, then there was a chance that keeping their forces as consolidated as possible was a more pressing concern than how quickly they could get the tunnels explored.

When we finally arrived at the last corner separating us from the remaining ant soldiers, it was obvious that we had a significant force waiting for us just around the bend. I'd been thinking in terms of ambush and booby-traps, but apparently I'd significantly underestimated the effect of my attacks back inside the compound before my men and I had been driven down to the basement.

Rather than continuing to rely on infrared as their main visual mode, the ants had detached the lights normally mounted to their rifles and set them up as improvised spotlights designed to light up the stretch of tunnel between us and them. Apparently one or more of the soldiers I'd killed back at the tunnel entrance had survived long enough to radio back to their comrades that they'd been under attack by someone who hadn't shown up on the infrared spectrum, and this was the solution they were hoping would allow them to see me coming.

Of course, I didn't find that out immediately. First I re-tasked my nanites away from my broken ribs and reactivated the thermal chameleon protocol that had served me so well up until now.

Once my body heat dissipated, I switched my goggles back over to the infrared spectrum and edged around the corner of the tunnel just far enough to take in what we were up against.

Tom and the others looked at me expectantly, but I wasn't sure what exactly to tell them. We were up against more than twenty highly-trained killers who were much better equipped than us, and who'd had time to dig in behind piles of dirt and rotted railroad ties that they'd obviously torn up in the time between when they'd arrived and when we managed to make it to them.

"As you can see, they've got lights set up from behind prepared positions. Based on the number of flashlights they've got mounted out there, we're up against at least a score of soldiers. Apparently they figured out that I can fool their thermal imaging, and this is how they're going to make sure I can't sneak up on them."

"I've been meaning to ask about that. How are you fooling the infrared mode on these devices?"

Tom scowled at the pathfinder we'd picked up as we'd left the noncombatants behind. "That information's need to know, and you don't have the need. Stop worrying about that and help come up with a way to get us out of here."

I couldn't help but smile at Tom. I'd been shocked enough when first Brennan and then Jax and Tyrell had been willing to trust me despite my origins, but never in a million years would I have expected the average member of

Brennan's guard to come out swinging in my defense.

"I'm not sure that we've got a ton of options. Even if there really are only twenty of them, they outnumber us by almost four to one, they are behind cover, and they may very well have more ammo than we do."

One of the other guards shrugged. "You're the brains of this operation. The rest of us are more than happy to have someone else tell us when and where to pull the trigger. Just being part of what Brennan was trying to build was reward enough all by itself. That hasn't changed, if you give the wrong orders and we all die that's nothing that we didn't have coming to us under our old lives. At least this way we got a chance to make a difference for a little while before ending up as worm food."

I had to swallow a couple of times to get my voice working normally. It shouldn't have been a surprise after my earlier conversation with Tom, but somehow it still was. I kept thinking that the people I met here in the city—in the compound at least—were the exception to the rule, but time and time again I was finding that the opposite was true. I had much more in common with the people Brennan had collected around him than I'd ever had with the people I'd known back home.

"Okay, here's what we're going to do. I need those lights shot out. We could exchange fire with these guys for hours and not manage to bring them down given all the armor they're wearing and the cover they've assembled, but if you guys can plunge this tunnel into darkness, I can end this. Who are your best shots?"

Tom and the other guy who'd spoken up in my defense—Steve—both raised their hands. I took the ant rifle back from the pathfinder and adjusted the red dot scope on it for the range we were going to be shooting at, and then handed it to Steve and showed him how it worked. It took only a few seconds to do the same for Tom, and then it was time to tell them my plan.

"There isn't enough cover on this end of the tunnel for us to pick the lights off unless we can come up with a way to equalize things."

I pointed at the pathfinder and one of the other guards who were still carrying the heavier rifles Brennan had turned out here in the city. "I need the two of you to lay down suppressive fire from this corner while Tom and I make a run for it. I don't care whether or not you hit anybody, but you need to be in the ballpark so that they'll keep their heads down, or the two of us will never make it."

I pointed at the heavy steel support that ran vertically between the ground and the top of the tunnel. "Tom, that's where I want you. You're going to be exposed, but you're also the only other one with body armor, so you're going to have to set up there. I'll continue on to the far side of the tunnel and set up in the crack in the wall right there."

Tom looked at me with confusion written large on his face. "That's no good, Skye. That crack will never provide good enough cover to keep you from getting killed. If the ants move to their left they'll be able to ricochet fire off the back wall and straight into your position."

I continued on as though I hadn't heard him. "As things stand right now, you should all be safe from their grenades. The range on a grenade launcher is only about half the distance between us and them, but if they start pushing this way you're going to have to force them back somehow without burning through all of your ammunition. That's a job for the three of you with the rifles Brennan gave you. They carry enough of a punch that you may be able to penetrate their body armor out to eighty or ninety yards.

"Tom and Steve will need to shoot out the lights. I know that seems like a tough shot at this distance, but even a near miss might be enough to send shards of rock into the glass of their lights. Once you knock out all of their lights, they'll have to switch to infrared. I want the five of you to do exactly the same thing. Turn off your lights and then slow down your rate of fire. Conserve your ammunition in case they pull out more lights, but other than that, I want to have your larger-caliber fire focused on the right side of their position while the left side gets shot at by Tom and Steve. That's important."

I turned as though the matter was settled, but Tom grabbed my arm. "What are you going to be doing?"

"I'm going to draw their fire and then I'm going to kill all of them."

Tom grabbed my arm. "What does that mean? You have to give us more to go on than that."

I pulled free of his grasp. "There isn't time. You all have your orders, if you follow them there's a chance that the people coming this direction who are counting on us to get them out of here may actually live to see the sun come up."

I turned the light on my rifle back on, amped up the armor protocol on the right side of my body as much as I could without crippling my speed, and then took off at a sprint towards the far wall.

I made it exactly four steps before the ants realized that they finally had a target. The hail of bullets I could hear headed my direction was entirely expected, but thankfully my men cut loose with full-automatic fire from all three of the guys with the heavier-caliber rifles.

I could hear Tom running behind me for all he was worth, and then the bullets started arriving. The wall to my left was almost perfectly perpendicular to the direction of the bullets being shot at me, which meant I had a lot less concern about ricochets taking me out than I otherwise would have, but I was still peppered by fragments of rock that were kicked loose from the force of the bullets slamming into the wall behind me.

THE DESTROYER

A bullet slammed into my shoulder and staggered me. There was a split second there where I was convinced I was going to lose my balance, and I saw my life flash before my eyes. The armor protocol I was running was good, but nothing was perfect and I knew if I hit the ground I would become an easy target and I wouldn't have just one bullet hit me, I'd have scores of them tearing into me.

At that point it would no longer be a question of *if* they could penetrate my skin, it would be a matter of *when*. The only thing keeping me alive was my speed and the covering fire I was receiving from the rest of my men.

I windmilled my arms, grimacing as a knife of pain stabbed through my ribs where they'd been broken, but it worked. I managed to get my left foot far enough forward and to the side to regain control of my center of gravity, and then I was only a few more steps away from the halfway point of my run.

Impossibly, Tom was gaining on me, but then the firing from behind me died out as quickly as it had started, and I realized I was going to have to stop behind the steel beam meant to shelter Tom. I was moving too fast to stop, I was going to overrun my destination, but the alternative was to slow down to the point where I'd get shot before I reached the safety of the massive I-beam. I did the only other thing I could.

Rather than slowing down I continued full speed ahead and let myself slam into the back of the metal beam in order to arrest my momentum. I knew I'd just added to the collection of bruises that my nanites still hadn't managed to deal with, but I was just glad that I hadn't broken anything. I turned around and used my arms to cushion Tom as he tried to repeat my reckless behavior. He still hit hard enough that he was going to be bruised just as spectacularly as I was, but we'd both made it safely behind the one piece of cover on this end of the tunnel.

"Are you crazy? The appropriate thing to do is to let the guys laying down cover fire get started before you run out into the open."

"I knew that wouldn't work. It was too far away and if I did it that way you probably would've been shot before you made it here. This way I drew the initial burst of fire and we both made it here alive."

I noted with morbid humor that I hadn't addressed his first question. I probably was out of my mind, but I just couldn't see any other way to get Lexis and the others out of here alive.

I pulled three of the magazines I'd taken off of dead ant soldiers out of the pockets in my pants and handed them to Tom. "Here, you're going to need these a lot more than I will. Go ahead and lay down about a half a clip worth of covering fire to kick the ball off so our buddies back there know when to start. Oh, don't forget to let me know when the lights are all out, but don't make such a production about it that the ants realize it's significant."

This time I waited for Tom to signal his readiness before sprinting away from the last real safety I was going to experience for the next several minutes.

It was worse this time, but I knew that was going to be the case even before I took my first step. Using covering fire to get to a better position was one of the oldest tricks in the book, and it was obvious that was what I was doing.

I took a shot in the leg at about the quarter mark, and then three more shots scattered between my shoulder and hip as I closed in on the two-thirds point. The bullets still carried a heckuva wallop even at that range, but I was better prepared for it this time and managed to avoid losing my balance right up until I was only one step away from my destination.

The last bullet took me in the helmet just behind my ear, and felt like it nearly broke my neck. I somehow managed to stumble into the crack that offered at least some protection from the incoming fire, and then took a moment to take stock of my condition.

The ballistic material of my helmet had managed to turn the bullet, but I could feel a big divot where the bullet had nearly penetrated the armor. Given the fact that I wasn't entirely sure that my armor protocol would be enough to save me if I took a bullet directly to the ear, the state of my helmet was plenty concerning, but I was equally worried about the blood trickling down my right leg.

It looked like my nanites had managed to turn the bullet, but they hadn't been quite equal to the task of doing so while preserving the integrity of my skin. I had a big crease that was bleeding at a rate that wasn't alarming in and of itself, but which I knew would result in a steady trickle of nanites exiting my body precisely at the time when I could least afford to be losing them.

I took a couple of steadying breaths and then shut off the armor protocol that was the only thing that kept me alive on my trip across the tunnel. Everything about my plan was dangerous—especially for me—but this was one of the most dangerous pieces. All it would take was for the right ricochet to hit me somewhere where my stolen armor didn't cover, or to hit my armor and penetrate, and I would be a dead woman.

I'd wanted to use a different plan, to find a way that didn't involve me running such insane risks, but there wasn't any other option. Even now the volume of fire coming from the other end of the tunnel was too heavy for Tom and Steve to get off anything even approaching aimed shots at the lights that we so desperately needed destroyed.

THE DESTROYER

I had to find a way to change the equation, and the only one I'd been able to come up with involved offering myself up as a target.

I'd activated the thermal chameleon protocol as soon as the armor protocol came down, but I didn't wait for my skin to start cooling down before I leaned out and started taking shots at the ants.

I didn't actually expect to hit anything at this range, not without more time to aim, but I did manage to take some of the pressure off of the rest of my guys. I ducked back into the crack in the wall and crouched down to try to minimize my target profile and increase my odds that any ricochets would hit my armor rather than unprotected flesh, but my real defense at this point was simply trying not to draw too much fire. Unfortunately, that was about to change.

I leaned back around the corner and fired off another couple shots, wincing as the return fire ricocheted over my head. I looked down at my hands and saw that they'd finally dropped down to the ambient temperature, which meant it was time to get everyone's attention. I stepped completely out from behind the crack in the wall where I'd been hiding and fired a full magazine at the ant's position with the selector set to automatic.

It was a tricky balance. All of this was for naught if I didn't manage to get them looking my direction, but if I didn't get my nanites re-tasked in time I wasn't going to survive. I ejected the spent magazine and slammed my last one home in one smooth motion and then concentrated my fire on one of the groups of flashlights. One of my shots must have gotten close enough to at least knock it off of the rock where they'd positioned it, and I felt a surge of satisfaction as I dropped my rifle and dove back into the crack, already shutting down the thermal chameleon protocol and turning on the armor protocol that I'd just finished abandoning.

Based on the sudden increase in the volume of fire headed in my direction, someone had finally realized that they were seeing bursts of fire coming from my position without a corresponding heat signature for the person holding the rifle. Now that they'd identified the individual who'd caused them so much grief when they'd tried to take the tunnel entrance, they were going to pull out all the stops in an attempt to eliminate me.

The only question now was whether or not my nanites would be able to re-task fast enough to keep me alive.

Even as I thought that, the ricochets started screaming in around me. Most of them were going well above my head, landing around what would've been chest level if I'd been standing, but I counted no less than four bullets impacting into my vest before the first one found unprotected flesh.

The protection I'd stolen from the dead soldiers ended just before the shoulder, and that first bullet slammed into my right arm just above the elbow with enough force that I half expected the bone there to break. It would've thrown me into the rock wall, but I was already huddled up as tight against that corner as I could possibly manage.

The only way this part of my plan could possibly work was if I was able to focus my nanites entirely on one half of my body, and my hope was that wedging myself tightly into the corner would make it so that I wouldn't have to worry about impacts anywhere other than along the back of my body. It was just a side benefit that doing so meant that all of the force transmitted by the bullets striking me couldn't knock me off balance.

Unfortunately, that didn't do anything for the pain, and I didn't dare redirect any of my nanites to deaden the nerve signals, not without reducing the strength of the armor protocol that was the only thing keeping me alive.

As the volume of fire slamming into me continued to increase, I tried to distract myself from the pain by focusing on the sound of Tom and Steve firing at the lights with metronome-like precision. The sooner they could get everything blacked out, the sooner I was going to be able to go after the men and women between me and the surface.

It sounded like my plan was working so far, which meant the only question was whether or not Tom and Steve could take out the lights before they either ran out of ammunition, or my armor protocol gave way under the incessant onslaught of bullets. I didn't even begin to have an understanding of how the nanites were turning my skin into the organic equivalent of Kevlar, but I was fairly sure that each time a bullet struck me, it was taking a toll on the nanites in that area of my body.

If that was true, then it was all just a question of how fast the nanites were being destroyed compared to how many nanites I had in my body, how fast the factory node in my chest could crank out more nanites, and how long I was going to have to remain in that crack. Even as I wondered how many nanites were being destroyed, I got a new readout in the corner of my vision, which was all the more incredible considering that my eyes were closed.

The readout consisted of nothing more than a series of pictographs with numbers next to them, but I had nothing but time with which to try to interpret them. It appeared as though the top number was signaling the rate at which my manufacturing node was turning out nanites, while the number below that was an estimate about how many were being killed, but there was no frame of reference to go along with the numbers. All I could assume was that they were using the same units, in which case it definitely appeared that the nanites were being destroyed more quickly than they were being replaced.

That theory was supported by the fact that the biggest number of all was a ninety-eight percent, which, even as I watched, dropped down to ninety-seven percent. The blood coming out of my leg had mostly trickled to a stop, which meant that the drop in overall nanite capacity could only be attributed to the destruction of nanites due to enemy fire.

I considered asking my neural computer for an estimate as to how much longer I had before the nanites would exhaust themselves to the point where the bullets would start penetrating my skin, but I didn't actually want to know. It seemed pointless to add yet another number floating in the darkness in front of me when there wasn't anything I could do to change my fate. It all depended on Tom and Steve.

The volume of fire coming into my position hadn't slackened at all, but I was still feeling pretty good about things until the first bullet penetrated the body armor covering my back.

It was stupid. I'd been so concerned about the degradation to my nanite-powered protection, but I'd never stopped to consider the fact that my body armor would also be subject to the same kind of erosion as time went on.

Luckily I'd had enough foresight to leave a thin layer of nanites over my entire back—even the sections covered by my body armor—but that had been nothing more than a precaution because I'd known full well that even the best body armor occasionally failed to stop a hit. The body armor didn't stop that particular round, but it did slow it down enough that it couldn't penetrate the skin over my right kidney. Still, it was a wake-up call.

I'd been focusing the majority of my nanites on my exposed skin, places the body armor didn't cover—especially my neck—but that was looking like a really sure way to get myself killed. I started re-tasking nanites, mentally spreading them over my back in a thicker layer that came at the expense of reducing my protection around my arms, shoulders, and legs. I was going to take some damage now, but it was that or risk the next bullet that hit my armor penetrating with enough force to make it inside my body.

I'd been praying that the bullet that'd penetrated my vest was some kind of fluke, but there'd been no way of knowing. I'd long since lost track of how many shots had torn into my back, but it turned out that my first penetrator was much less of an outlier than I'd been hoping.

Bullets continued to come screaming off of the back wall like a hot, lead rainfall, and they were getting through my armor with worrisome regularity now. So far nothing had managed to tear through my skin—underneath my armor or otherwise—but the readout was down to ninety-two percent already, and I was pretty sure I would have already been bleeding if not for the fact that the bullets hitting me lost a significant amount of their kinetic energy during their hundred-yard flight to the back side of the tunnel and then their subsequent collision with the rock face that was directing them into me.

The readout continued to drop. I was at eighty-five percent when the first bullet hit with enough force to cut through my skin and ricochet off of my shoulder blade. I was now faced with an impossible choice. The blood flowing down my arm was only a trickle, but more bullets were going to get through, which meant I could either maintain my armor protocol and slowly bleed to death, or I could re-task some of my nanites away to try to heal my wound.

Instead I chose a third option. I pulled my combat knife out of my boot and used it to slice the inside of my right arm. The trickle of blood coming down from my shoulder quickly turned into something much more dangerous, and I was left to hope that I'd timed things right.

There wasn't anything I could do about my shoulder—not without risking having my hand blown off by the next bullet that hit that location—but I could've stemmed the bleeding from my arm if that had been part of my plan. Instead I watched the readout drop even further. In theory my nanites were all firmly anchored to my dermis rather than swimming around in my blood, but reality was rarely as clean as that. I was down to seventy-five percent, and it was dropping even more quickly than it had been a moment before, but the pool of blood to the right of me was growing quite nicely.

Reaching over with my right hand and forcing the blood to move away from me was a risk, but no more so than anything else I'd done so far. I didn't want to lose my hand, but I was going to lose a lot more than that if the ants didn't see enough blood soon to convince themselves that I was dead.

I could hear Tom and Steve continuing to take shots at the lights. I was down to fifty percent when it finally happened. There was a short pause in the shooting, and when it resumed none of the bullets were ricocheting in my direction. I'd done it—I'd convinced them that they'd killed the bogeyman who'd decimated the rest of their force just hours earlier, and I'd managed it without actually dying. The only question was whether Tom and Steve had managed to take out all the lights. If they hadn't done it by now, then their odds of managing it now that they were under heavier fire weren't good.

"How are we looking, Tom?"

I used the lowest voice I thought would carry to him over the roar of gunfire, but I was still worried that the ants would somehow overhear me. To distract myself from that worry I pulled my right arm back in and applied pressure to the cut I'd made. I considered re-tasking my nanites to deal with the damage in my arm and shoulder, but if somebody decided to take a shot at me, I was going to need what was left of my armor protocol, tattered though it was.

"How are you still alive?"

"That's not important right now. I need you to focus on the mission. Have you guys taken out all of the lights yet?"

"No, there's still one more set of lights that we haven't managed to hit yet. The angle's bad, and now that you've convinced them that you're dead it's getting hard to get off a shot."

The readout in the corner of my vision dropped down to forty-nine percent. I re-tasked the nanites to healing all of the breaches in my skin. I didn't have any other choice, not if I was going to have anything left with which to make my move once the cavern was plunged into darkness. I turned around to present undamaged armor across my chest to any ricochets that might come after me, and just hoped that would be enough.

"You guys have got to take that light out for me, Tom. Everything depends on it, and ideally it needs to happen before both sides have shot themselves dry. There's no guarantee this is all that's left of the ants, and even if it is, we're not going to be completely home free once we make it to the surface.

"Brennan's territory was full of enforcers when the bombardment started, and guys like that aren't just going to sit back once the dust settles. They're going to try to rebuild their own personal little fiefdom out of whatever the ants have left here. We're going to need enough firepower to defend ourselves if we're going to have any chance of saving those noncombatants."

"What do you want me to do, Skye?"

"Whatever it takes. Get the rest of the guys to lay down full-auto fire to force the ants back behind cover, and then you and Steve need to make sure those lights go out. I'll never get close enough to kill that many soldiers if they can see me coming, and that's exactly what will happen unless we can force all of them to switch over to thermal imaging. This is for the whole ball of wax, Tom. The better part of a thousand civilians are depending on you to make that shot."

There was a pause that stretched out so long I almost thought Tom was going to refuse my order, but when he finally responded his voice was steady. "I understand. Give me a second to set it up with everybody else."

I caught the fringes of Tom's orders to the rest of the guards, but he was yelling in the other direction so it was hard to hear much of anything over the ongoing thunder of bullets hitting the back of the tunnel and ricocheting away in all directions. The bleeding from my arm had stopped by the time Tom and the others made their move.

THE DESTROYER

There was half a second of silence in our end of the tunnel and then everything lit up as all three guardsmen with the heavier-caliber rifles stepped around the corner and opened up on the ant position. My goggles were switched over to infrared, so I was easily able to see Tom and Steve both roll out from behind their cover and begin trying to shut off the last remaining cluster of lights.

They hadn't been kidding when they'd said that they were both expert marksman. Their shots were maybe half a second apart, and after only four shots a piece Steve cheered and rolled back to the other side so that he was no longer exposed. Tom did the same, but he moved more slowly, and when he spoke again his voice was weak and shaky.

"We got it, Skye. The last light is down, and we'll do what we can to plunge them back into darkness if they get one of them working again. Go ahead and make your move whenever you're ready."

I didn't need to see the slowly expanding pool of red underneath him to know what had happened. He'd been shot, and he didn't have nanites to help slow down the bleeding. Unlike Steve, Tom had been armored, but this time that hadn't been enough.

"How badly are you hit?"

"Bad enough that there's not much point in conserving my ammo anymore."

"Tie it off."

Tom looked directly at me and shook his head. "It won't work. I didn't get shot just once, I got hit multiple times. My left arm isn't working very well, and the bullet that went into my shoulder feels like it traveled all the way down to my hip before it stopped. The internal bleeding is going to finish me off no matter what else I do."

"Hold on, I'll come over there and get pressure on all of your entry wounds."

"If you do that, I might as well shoot you myself. Your plan obviously depends on everybody thinking that you're dead. If you come over here that all goes down the toilet."

I re-tasked my nanites to activate the thermal camouflage, but I had no idea if it was even going to work given how few nanites I had left.

"No, it can still work. I'll make myself invisible to thermal imaging and then come over and get you."

Tom chuckled, but it sounded like even just doing that nearly caused him to pass out. "Sure, but then what happens if you take a round yourself? I'm guessing that you can't maintain your invisibility and make yourself bulletproof at the same time, or it seems like you would've done so already. They're not shooting spit wads at me over here."

He was right—as much as I wanted to argue with him, he was right. Now that the ants had crossed me off of the list of threats, the volume of fire being thrown at our remaining two positions was absolutely lethal. I could tell Tom to order another round of suppressive fire from the guards over at Steve's position, but there was no guarantee that Tom would pass the order on. Even worse, there was no guarantee even if he did so that it would be enough to get me safely to his side.

When you added in the fact that then I was going to need to find a way to get back out from behind the steel beam that was sheltering him, my odds of avoiding being shot plunged to something uncomfortably close to zero.

Apparently I'd been silent for too long. "You know I'm right, Skye. Go do your thing and stop worrying about me."

"I'm tired of losing people, Tom. It's been less than three hours and I've already lost almost all of you."

"Yeah, but it's like I said before. At least we had a chance to die working towards something other than lining some warlord's pockets. That's a hell of a lot better than anybody else from my home territory ever managed."

I looked down at my arm and saw that it had dropped to something only a few degrees hotter than the ambient air temperature. The readout was showing what appeared to be zero nanites being lost on an ongoing basis. I was up to fifty percent of normal nanite capacity, but I was getting the feeling that it was going to be a while before the manufacturing node in my chest made good on my losses so far—even assuming that was still possible with the amount of heavy metals remaining in my system. It was now or never.

The barrel of my rifle was still hot from the little bit of shooting I'd done earlier, so I left it behind as I stood and stepped out from behind my cover. I'd done my best to construct another three-dimensional map inside my head based off of glimpses of things that I'd registered while my goggles had still been set to lowlight mode.

That meant that I had at least some idea of what kind of terrain I was trying to traverse, but it was still a painstaking, slow undertaking. I moved in fits and starts from one piece of cover to another while holding my breath. Once I got somewhere that gave me a chance of obscuring the plume of heat as I exhaled, I hyperventilated in an attempt to bring my core temperature down to something that wouldn't cause my brain to stop functioning, and then I picked out the next bit of half-remembered cover from my mental map, took a deep breath, and did it all over again.

The closer I got to the ants, the more dangerous things became. The readout was still sitting at fifty percent, which meant that my chameleon protocol wasn't getting any better. With every step forward it became that much more likely that the bad guys would see the faint blue outline of a person walking toward them or, failing that, see the heat I emitted when I breathed out.

Even if that didn't happen, I was convinced with every step I took that the ants were going to produce another set of lights, which would allow them to easily see me approaching them. Tom had said that he and Steve would do their best to shoot out the lights if that happened, but I was under no illusions there. By now it was almost certain that Tom was dead, and shooting at something as small as those lights while simultaneously under fire himself meant that Steve was unlikely to manage a hit as quickly as I would need for it to happen.

Once you added in the fact that Steve was doing exactly as I'd instructed and occasionally taking a shot at the left side of the ants' position, it was looking more and more certain that I was going to die from a bullet in the back of my head if the ants didn't get me before then.

There was no good cover left between me and the ants, so I moved all the way over to the left wall and went as far as I could before stopping to breathe. This time I turned my back to the ants and tried to direct the hot air in such a way that my body would screen the worst of the heat plume. I didn't know if it would work, but nobody shot me, so I took a deep breath and turned around so I could continue forward.

I was getting close enough that I had to worry about the sound of my movements alerting my enemies, which just slowed things down even more, but I continued to make steady progress as both sides reduced the volume of fire they were hurling back and forth at each other.

I was less than a dozen yards away from the bad guys when one of Steve's shots came screaming out of the darkness and took me in the right leg. The pain was beyond intense, but I not only managed not to scream, I slapped my hands over the entry and exit wound in an effort to keep the blood pouring out of my leg from creating a recognizable heat signature.

I could no longer afford to continue with the slow, measured pace I'd been employing up to that point. Without nanites tasked to seal off the holes in my leg, it was only a matter of time before the blood made it past my hands enough for the bad guys to see me coming.

I took off at a run, counting on speed to get me to my first target before anyone could react to the sound of my approach. I'd already been at the end of my ability to hold my breath, but I pushed my limits, refusing to exhale until I was flying over the top of the improvised barricade housing the ant to the furthest left of their firing line.

I whipped my knife out of its sheath and slammed it home in the first soldier's neck. The other two soldiers hiding behind the same barricade couldn't help but hear my first victim's rifle hit the ground, but I was on them even before they could yell. I cut the throat of the closest guy as I blew past him on my way forward to punch the next guy in the throat.

I wanted so badly to pick up a weapon and use it to gun down the remaining seventeen ants, but I knew that would be a mistake. Regardless of how well my chameleon protocol had held up, there was no way to miss a bright pink glowing barrel that had shot off the better part of a hundred rounds since we'd started this standoff.

I was going to have to do this up close and personal, fighting men who were going to be faster and stronger than me. The element of surprise was the one advantage I had and I was going to have to milk it for as long as I could.

I finished off the guy I'd punched while he was still clawing at his throat for breath that was never going to come, and then dropped down so I could breathe without being seen. My core temperature was getting dangerously high, but there simply wasn't time to stop and try to bleed off some of the waste heat that was building up underneath the surface of my skin. I had only seconds until the ants closest to me started wondering why this gun pit had gone silent.

I rose to my feet again and started forward in an arc so that I would come at my next group of enemies more from behind rather than directly from the side. I spared a moment to hope that Steve and the rest of the guys were smart enough to have seen my first batch of victims drop and adjust their fire so as to not take me out by accident.

The second gun pit housed four more soldiers, but I ruthlessly dispatched them almost as quickly as I had the men in the first emplacement. I used my knowledge of the human body and my familiarity with standard-issue ant body armor to strike in spots that were almost guaranteed to render the target instantly unconscious, but that was more precaution against the rest of their squad rather than the other members of the gun pit.

I severed the renal artery on the fourth guy, being careful to stand to one side so that I wouldn't get coated in warm blood that would ruin my thermal invisibility, at nearly the same time as the guy furthest away from him finished falling to the ground. I held my hand over his mouth for the two seconds it took for his body to go limp, and then leaned him forward over the makeshift wall in front of him before reaching around and sliding his knife free of its sheath on the front of his body armor.

Based on my preliminary headcount I still had thirteen enemies to eliminate, and I cautioned myself not to get sloppy or overconfident. My initial success by no means guaranteed that I would be able to continue to cut through more than a dozen trained, hardened killers without getting killed in the process.

THE DESTROYER

Despite that, I took out four more targets before anyone noticed just how quiet my side of the firing line had become. I saw the soldier who'd become suspicious start to turn his head toward me, and did the only thing I could think of. I hurled my stolen knife forward, sending it flying end over end to embed itself six inches into the side of the soldier's neck.

I threw myself forward as I mentally re-tasked my nanites to increasing my speed and strength. There was no conceivable way for me to kill the remaining soldiers by myself, but killing the soldier who'd been just about to raise the alarm was only going to buy me a second at best before someone noticed him slumping over his rifle.

I took out my next two targets with my knife while they were turning away from me to check on their companion who'd just taken a knife to his neck. I didn't make them quiet kills this time, partially because I was in a hurry and partially because I figured anything I could do to increase the confusion I was creating was going to pay dividends.

I slammed my knife into the chest of the second of my two latest kills, but rather than letting him hit the ground, I hauled him to his feet with my left hand as I released my knife and grabbed his rifle with my other. He wasn't just a normal rifleman, I could tell by the weight of his weapon that it had a grenade launcher mounted to it, and I wasted no time holding down both triggers as I sprayed both bullets and grenades up the line of soldiers who were only then starting to turn in my direction.

It was a tactic of desperation. Aiming with only one hand like I was, I was unlikely to hit any of my enemies on the few parts of their bodies not covered by armor, and the grenades spewing forth from my weapon were aimed at spots much too close to me for there to be any chance I could escape the fringes of the blast when they finally went off.

Dozens of bullets impacted on my human shield as the ants stitched their fire upwards toward my head, and then I ducked down behind the protection of the soldier's torso a split second before the grenades went off in one long rolling cacophony of destruction.

My nanites were augmenting my strength by that point, but it was taking everything I had to keep nearly two hundred pounds of dead weight dangling in front of me, and the force of so many bullets being transmitted through my shield into me had already sent me staggering backwards. The concussive blast from so many grenades going off at once knocked me to the ground and left both my ears and head ringing.

The display that my supercomputer layered over top of my normal vision was flashing now and reporting a twenty percent drop in the number of functioning nanites inside of my system. I wanted nothing so badly as to just lie there and wait for death to come for me, but I knew that wasn't an option. Too many people were depending on me and I'd given Brennan my promise—vicariously, but a promise nevertheless—that I would find a way to get his people to safety.

I pushed what was left of the corpse I'd been holding off to one side, and then re-tasked my nanites to try to deal with the dangerous amounts of blood streaming out of my body. Somehow my combat knife had survived the blast, still embedded in my victim's chest, and I pulled it out of the body as I forced myself to my feet.

I desperately needed to stop and bandage up my wounds before the last of my nanites were forced out of my body in a vain attempt to stem the bleeding, but I couldn't let myself do that until I'd made sure of all of the soldiers. They'd all mostly been even closer to the blast points than I'd been, but they'd been starting out with pristine body armor and nanites that were automatically programmed to put triaging wounds ahead of all other priorities.

As incredible as it felt given my current state, I had every reason to believe that some of the soldiers would make a full recovery if given enough time for the nanites to seal off the ghastly wounds they'd no doubt suffered from my grenades. I had to make sure of them, even if it killed me. I moved from soldier to soldier cutting throats or otherwise opening up arteries that I knew even nanites couldn't fully repair before their hosts bled out.

I was surprised to find the detachment's commander at the very end of the line of men and women. Even more astonishing given the fact that it looked like one of the grenades had gone off only inches away from him, he was still alive. Despite all of the death and gore I'd been exposed to since arriving in the city, I couldn't bring myself to dwell on the wreckage of the bottom half of his body as I pulled my knife back to end his life.

"What are you doing? You're obviously one of us, you couldn't have done what you did without nanites, but you're helping a bunch of mindless grubbers. You should be ashamed of yourself."

"That's where you're wrong. I'm not one of you. I never was. It's just taken me seventeen years to realize that."

I killed him with the last of my strength and then collapsed to the ground next to him. I knew I needed to try to stop myself from bleeding out, but my entire body had simply become too heavy to move.

Chapter 11

I came to as Steve and one of the other guards carried me up to the surface just behind our lead scouting elements. Apparently they'd started my direction as soon as the grenades went off despite knowing that there was a chance I still hadn't managed to kill all of the ants. It was a good thing they had—if they'd arrived even a minute or two later, or been a tad slower applying first-aid to the worst of my wounds, I probably wouldn't have survived.

I woke up disoriented, unsure how much time had passed, but rather than the small advance group of guardsmen that I'd been expecting to find, I could hear hundreds of feet trudging along behind me. I wanted to order the civilians to fall back so that they wouldn't get caught in an ambush if there were more ants waiting for us at the surface, but I was just too weak to get the words out.

I did manage to flop my head to the side enough to see that more than twenty of the noncombatants had armed themselves with weapons taken from what I hoped was my final batch of victims for quite some time.

Spunk and Tiny were holding Lexis' hands as they walked on the other side of Steve. I caught them looking at me and their eyes were incredibly wide. It made me sad to see them look at me that way. I'd been so worried when I'd first found them that they were going to be scarred by the things I had to do to get them safely to the compound. I'd been relieved when I'd been able to hand them off to Lexis and they'd seemed none the worse for the wear. I should've known that eventually being around me would affect them negatively.

It was just one more way in which there was no going back to the person I'd been when I'd jumped out of that plane so many days before. I never could have prevented Spunk and Tiny's loss of innocence any more than I could replace my own.

Someone swore up ahead, and then familiar voices were yelling for everyone to get back inside the tunnel.

"What's going on? Get me closer to the front, please, I need to know what's going on."

It took me two tries to get my voice to work well enough for Steve to hear me, but once he did he stopped backing up and gestured for the guard who was helping him to do as I'd ordered.

The pathfinder Tom had dressed down earlier in the tunnels met us a few feet from the door to the building we were standing inside of.

"It's all been for nothing. I thought after everything we've been through that all we were going to have to worry about was a few dozen enforcers, but that's not what is waiting for us out there. It's some kind of flying vehicle, something belonging to the ants. I knew they could fly, but I never would've believed that they could get something so big into the air."

Something inside of me died when I heard those words. He had to be talking about the dropship, which meant that Brennan had failed. All of the ant aircraft incorporated significant stealth technology. It was designed to protect the military against any grubbers who managed to get a working radar installation up and running, but it also meant that once Brennan and the others disabled the dropship's transponder, they would effectively be invisible as long as they moved under the cover of clouds.

Even despite that, hanging around here would be a death sentence. The dropship could defeat run-of-the-mill surveillance, but it couldn't hide from the best surveillance satellites under the Citizen-President's control, not when there were so many of them pointed directly at this area, and not when they already knew the aircraft was here.

There was only one explanation for the dropship hovering outside of our building, and that was that Brennan's attack on it had failed.

"Carry me out there."

"Skye, are you crazy? There's absolutely nothing you can do against something like that, especially not when you can't even stand unaided."

I looked over at Lexis and gave her a sad smile. "You're right that there's nothing I can do to save us, but there's still something I can do—something I have to do. Please, Steve, carry me out there and then the two of you can come back in here and lead everyone back down into the tunnels. It won't save you—not long-term at least—but you can make them dig you out. You can at least try to take a few more of them with you along the way."

Steve looked hesitantly over to Lexis, and then nodded and carried me out to the road where I could easily see the dropship hovering over the smoking wreckage that had been left behind by the high-altitude bombardment.

Steve and the other guard sat me down with my back to the building and then went back inside. I waited a few seconds to gather my strength and then cleared my throat.

"I have important information that needs to be shared with every franchised citizen. We have all been duped for the last hundred and fifty years. The Founder isn't dead, he's been controlling our Society under many different guises. We've all been working for decades in the pursuit of nanite technology sufficiently advanced to extend human life indefinitely, but it's already in existence."

The dropship started to drift towards me, confirming that they had a directional mic pointed at me, but not giving me any indication whether or not my words were having the desired effect.

"I don't expect any of you to believe me just based on nothing more than my words, but if you examine me you will find that I'm speaking the truth. I have nanites swimming inside my bloodstream that are much more advanced than anything given even to the military, and they aren't some cutting-edge development, they are technology that's been around since before the Desolation.

"Don't let the Founder continue to make our lives meaningless. For once in your lives, make your own decisions and follow a path other than the one that he set out for you."

A massive bay on the dropship began to open, revealing armed soldiers lined up as though ready to act as a firing squad. It was a bad sign, but I refused to admit defeat. I'd said everything I could think of to say, so I simply squared my jaw and refused to look away from my captors.

A second later one of those armed figures threw himself out of the dropship bay and plummeted to the ground for several dozen yards before his grav chute deployed itself in an invisible surge of power. He landed on the asphalt a hundred yards away from me and sprinted in my direction with speed that no normal human could have hoped to match.

I refused to believe what my eyes were telling me, not because I didn't want it to be true, but because after everything I'd been through it seemed very possible I was hallucinating. It wasn't until Brennan swept me into his arms that I finally allowed myself to believe it was really happening.

"You made it. Tyrell and Jax kept telling me that there was no way you were going to be able to fight your way out of there, but I refused to believe that you were dead. I made them keep the dropship here waiting for you. Thank you for saving my life yet again, and for bringing Lexis and the rest of my people safely through an impossible situation, but most of all thank you for coming back to me again."

I opened my mouth, unsure what I was going to say, but Brennan didn't give me a chance to say anything. He kissed me.

For a few seconds everything else ceased to matter. My body didn't hurt, and I wasn't worried about the future. All I cared about was that I finally knew exactly how he felt about me, and my feelings—feelings it'd taken me a long time to admit even to myself—were reciprocated.

As hard as it was to believe, my people had helped distract the ants for long enough that Tyrell and Jax had managed to capture an ant dropship. That was an almost inconceivable achievement, one that was guaranteed to bring the full might of the ant military machine against us.

We were safe for the moment, but we weren't out of the woods by any means. The mobile command center that had just destroyed most of the city was still floating tens of thousands of feet overhead, still able to rain down destruction on us once the dust from the earlier strikes finished settling enough for the personnel up there to realize something was wrong. The dropship was the most immediate threat, but even if we managed to evade it, we would still be fugitives. We would be fugitives with resources that hadn't been seen since before the desolation, though, and that might make all the difference.

I could see a long, dangerous fight stretching out before us—one that might kill us all at some point—but for now Brennan was safe, and I'd managed to save Lexis and the others. All of the fighting and killing had been worth it.

Acknowledgements

I had no idea what I was getting into when I started writing The Society. With each book in the series, the process of trying to get my ideas into a coherent vision has become harder, and without the help of a large number of people The Destroyer probably wouldn't have ever become a reality.

My editors (Amy Jirsa-Smith and RJ Locksley) both did exemplary work when it came to whipping my rough draft into something with far fewer errors than the version I handed them—thank you both!

My advance readers continued to gamely provide feedback and proofing for The Destroyer despite the fact that it was a big departure from the kind of stuff that many of them most enjoy reading. I'm grateful to all of them for their ongoing help and support. In no particular order they are: Mom, Dad, Matthew, Shalese, Lachele, Mimi, Mark, Kim, Janelle, Jenine, Mei and Heather.

I would also like to express thanks to Merissa at http://archaeolibrarianologist.blogspot.com/ for her ongoing efforts to get the word out about my books, all of the members of my Launch Team (you guys and gals are awesome), and all of you readers who take the time to tell your friends and family about my books.

Finally, as always, the biggest thanks goes to my wife, Katie. Writing The Destroyer ushered in a particularly trying time for me professionally and I couldn't have continued doing what I do without her help. Thank you Katie.

About the Author

Dean Murray is a prolific author with dozens of titles across multiple pen names and more than half a million copies of his work currently in circulation.

Dean started reading seriously in the second grade due to a competition and has spent most of the subsequent three decades lost in other people's worlds.

Things worsened, or improved depending on your point of view, when he first started experimenting with writing while finishing up his accounting degree. These days Dean has a wonderful wife and two lovely daughters to keep him rather more grounded, but the idea of bringing others along with him as he meets interesting new people in universes nobody else has ever seen tends to drag him back to his computer on a fairly regular basis.

Keep up to speed on Dean's latest projects at deanwrites.com.

Stone Heart

Dani's new home isn't just another stopover in a long chain of places she'll never see again, it's the home of both Caine and Jerek, two guys like nobody she's ever met before. One represents the best friend she's been hungering for, and the other represents something much more.

It should be the perfect recipe for a fairytale, but Caine and Jerek live in a dark, shadowy world and one of them is hiding secrets that will change everything, secrets that relate directly to Dani.

Reborn

True love never dies.

A new arrival at Selene's high school is about to turn her entire world upside down. She's never met anyone so attractive—or so mysterious—before this, but Jace's unyielding insistence that they've known each other for decades can't be denied—not given how familiar he feels to her.

In the hidden world of gods and fairies what you don't know can get you killed faster than anything else and only those you love have any chance of saving you.

Broken

Adri Paige's arrival in Sanctuary thrusts her into a dangerous, shadowy world most people don't believe exists, and places her in the middle of a war between darkly handsome Alec Graves and charismatic Brandon Worthingfield that threatens to consume the entire town.

On the surface, both Alec and Brandon are nothing more than average high-school guys, but as Adri is pulled ever more deeply into their conflict she realizes that one of them wants to kill her. Adri needs to decide who to trust before her time runs out once and for all.

The Greater Darkenss

Dean writing as Eldon Murphy

Something powerful is stirring in the darkness. Something so ancient that even creatures who've been alive for hundreds of years have long since discounted this new threat as nothing more than myth.

Normal humans will be caught in the crossfire, but then that's always the way of things. Geoffrey has no memory of his past life or any idea how to survive in the violent, dangerous world in which he's trapped. Despite his best efforts, he's about to find himself in the middle of a conflict that threatens to sweep away everything, and everyone he's been fighting so hard to protect.